"Why are you moving, Mardi? Bitter memories?" Cain asked.

Mardi shrugged. Bitter memories? Yes…she still felt bitter that her husband had left his family so badly in debt, and equally bitter—more bitter than heartbroken—about his affair with Cain's wife.

"Look, I'm here because of Benjamin, my son," Cain said. "Keeping Ben away from Nicky hasn't worked out. There's a week left before school starts. If we allow the boys to see each other, a week should be long enough, hopefully, for them to get over their obsession with each other…."

"I don't think it's a good idea—"

"You're being very hard on the boys…." he argued.

She reluctantly agreed. But it wasn't the memories she was worried about. It had more to do with her obsessions—hers with a tall, handsome, potently attractive man with cobalt eyes named *Cain Templar!*

Dear Reader,

Summer's finally here! Whether you'll be lounging poolside, at the beach, or simply in your home this season, we have great reads packed with everything you enjoy from Silhouette Romance—tenderness, emotion, fun and, of course, heart-pounding romance—plus some very special surprises.

First, don't miss the exciting conclusion to the thrilling ROYALLY WED: THE MISSING HEIR miniseries with Cathie Linz's *A Prince at Last!* Then be swept off your feet—just like the heroine herself!—in Hayley Gardner's *Kidnapping His Bride*.

Romance favorite Raye Morgan is back with *A Little Moonlighting*, about a tycoon set way off track by his beguiling associate who wants a family to call her own. And in Debrah Morris's *That Maddening Man*, can a traffic-stopping smile convince a career woman—and single mom—to slow down...?

Then laugh, cry and fall in love all over again with two incredibly tender love stories. Vivienne Wallington's *Kindergarten Cupids* is a very different, highly emotional story about scandal, survival and second chances. Then dive right into Jackie Braun's *True Love, Inc.*, about a professional matchmaker who's challenged to find her very sexy, very cynical client his perfect woman. Can she convince him that she already has?

Here's to a wonderful, relaxing summer filled with happiness and romance. See you next month with more fun-in-the-sun selections.

Happy reading!

Mary-Theresa Hussey

Mary-Theresa Hussey
Senior Editor

Please address questions and book requests to:
Silhouette Reader Service
U.S.: 3010 Walden Ave., P.O. Box 1325, Buffalo, NY 14269
Canadian: P.O. Box 609, Fort Erie, Ont. L2A 5X3

Kindergarten Cupids

VIVIENNE WALLINGTON

SILHOUETTE *Romance*®

Published by Silhouette Books

America's Publisher of Contemporary Romance

SILHOUETTE BOOKS

ISBN 0-373-19596-6

KINDERGARTEN CUPIDS

Copyright © 2002 by Vivienne Wallington

This edition published by arrangement with Harlequin Books S.A.

Visit Silhouette at www.eHarlequin.com

Printed in U.S.A.

Books by Vivienne Wallington

Silhouette Romance

Claiming His Bride #1515
Kindergarten Cupids #1596

VIVIENNE WALLINGTON

is an Australian living in Melbourne, Victoria, in an area with lots of trees, birds and parkland. She has been happily married to John, her real-life hero, for over forty years and they have a married son and daughter and five grandchildren who provide inspiration for her books. Vivienne worked as a librarian for many years, but was always writing, as well, eventually having a children's book published. After two more years, she gave up writing for children to concentrate on romance. She has written nineteen Harlequin Romance titles under the pseudonym Elizabeth Duke, and is now writing for Silhouette under her real name. Her favorite hobbies are reading, research, family and travel.

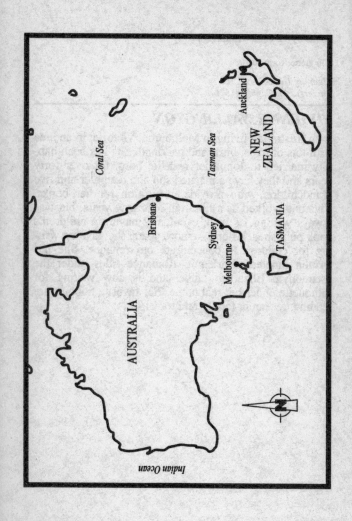

Chapter One

Watching from the kitchen as her son, Nicky, romped on the back lawn with Scoots, his beloved black Labrador, Mardi Sinclair wondered how she could bear to take her son away from the home and the rambling garden he'd come to love. But she had no choice. The house was sold now, and she had a month to find another place to live—a smaller place in a less expensive area. A house or flat that she could rent, not buy.

But with a five-year-old son, an ailing grandfather and a large, exuberant dog, it wasn't proving easy.

She caught her breath as she saw her son's purple-framed glasses go flying as he rolled on the grass with Scoots. *Oh, no, please, no, not another pair of broken glasses!*

Mardi rushed outside.

But Nicky was already pulling them back on. "They're not broken, Mummy." He shot her a triumphant grin as he patted his glasses back into place. He'd hated wearing them at first, but he'd grown used to them, and now wore them with pride.

And Mardi was proud of her brave son. She loved him to pieces. His astigmatism had improved already, and in a few years, if the eye specialist was right, he would be able to throw away his glasses. Perhaps, soon, his infected tonsils would be history, too.

She caught him in her arms and hugged him tight. "That's good, darling. That's great."

"Mummy…" Nicky looked up at her with beseeching gray eyes, the sunlight glinting on his grass-smudged lenses. "Can we ask Ben over to play tomorrow?"

Mardi's heart wrenched. She'd lost count of the times Nicky had asked about his friend Benjamin Templar since his father had died and the kindergarten had broken up for the long summer holidays. She'd made excuses to him each time. She did so again.

"We have to look for a new home, darling." She'd tried to explain to him that they couldn't afford such a big house or garden anymore, now that Daddy had gone to heaven, but it was hard for a five-year-old to understand. "We'll try to find a house near a nice park or a playground, where you and Scoots can run around." They were unlikely to have a spacious lawn or even a garden at their new place.

"Can Ben come to the park with us?" Nicky asked.

Mardi sighed. Ben, always Ben. Since the day he'd started at St. Mark's kindergarten, when they moved into their new home last August, the two boys had been inseparable. Ben, the older by three months and quite a bit taller, had taken on a protective role, shielding Nicky from any taunts and teasing by the other children. And Nicky's quick mind and easygoing manner had often saved Ben from trouble, drawing the boys closer and cementing their friendship. They'd been looking forward to starting school together this year. Who would look out for her son when he moved to another school?

"Look, why don't you go and ask Grandpa to have a game of snakes and ladders with you before dinner?" Diversion, Mardi had found, often did the trick in taking Nicky's mind off Benjamin Templar.

"Grandpa's having a snooze."

"Well, it's time you came in and had a bath anyway," she said, and frowned as the front doorbell rang. "Oh, heck, who could that be at this hour?" Not the estate agent, she hoped. What a time to want to discuss houses for rent, just as her carrot cake and cottage pie were due to come out of the oven. "Keep an eye on Scoots, Nicky. I'll just run and see."

Instead of going back inside to answer the door, she sprinted around the side of the attractive Federation-style house—the house they'd been in for less than six months and now had to leave—and bounded up the steps to the front veranda.

She faltered. It wasn't the balding estate agent standing at her front door. It was a tall, dark-haired stranger in a beautifully cut business suit.

As he turned to face her, revealing a pair of intensely blue eyes in a strong, square-jawed face, she pulled up short, shock momentarily paralyzing her.

It was *him*. The man she'd almost collided with at the kindergarten a few months ago—another parent, she'd assumed, who'd already dropped off his child. How could she ever forget those eyes, that face? Or her own humiliating reaction?

As he'd stepped aside, their eyes had clashed, and in that heart-stopping second she'd felt a jolt of sexual awareness that had shocked her, an electrifying sensation she'd never felt before, not even in her happier days with Darrell.

Her face flamed at the embarrassing memory.

And now here he was again, at her *home*. She gulped

hard, hardly able to believe her eyes. He looked just the same as she remembered him from that unforgettable morning, just as riveting with those compelling blue eyes, the slashing black brows, the firm sensual mouth and the broadest shoulders she'd ever seen. And just as sexy and stylish in another superb designer suit.

As her heart fluttered—what was he doing *here?*—her mind raced ahead, seeking answers. Again he had no child with him. Maybe he wasn't a kindergarten parent after all, but one of St Mark's teachers. Not at the kindergarten—she knew all the teachers there—but at the adjoining primary school, where Nicky was to have started school in a weeks' time.

She hadn't told the school yet that she'd sold her house and would be moving away from this area, possibly too far away to keep Nicky on at St. Mark's.

The bitter truth was, she couldn't afford to keep her son at a private school. She would have to send Nicky to a state school this year, in whatever suburb they moved to. And she'd have to find full-time work for herself—they couldn't manage on what she'd been earning last year, working two days a week in the office of a girls' school, or doing the menial jobs she'd managed to scrounge during the holidays.

"Mrs. Sinclair?" His voice cut the silence.

Mardi swallowed again, wishing she didn't feel so hot and flustered after her unladylike sprint round the house, or so messy, in her flour-covered shorts and T-shirt. The flour was probably on her cheeks and in her hair, as well.

She nodded, trying to maintain her dignity. He'd shown no sign of recognizing her from their fleeting encounter last September. Hardly surprising, she reflected, since she'd been respectably clean and tidy then, and neatly dressed, ready for her part-time job.

"Mardi," she said automatically, in a voice that wobbled slightly.

An imperceptible nod. It occurred to her that there was little warmth in the blue eyes, although his manner and tone of voice—he had a deep, pleasant voice, she noted—were courteous enough. Courteous, without being friendly. She had the distinct impression he was making an *effort* to be pleasant.

Surely a teacher at St. Mark's would have a warmer, friendlier approach.

The firm lips moved again, uttering the last name in the world that she'd expected to hear, or would have wanted to hear.

"Cain Templar." His strong jaw jutted a trifle. "I'm here because of my son, Benjamin."

She stared. He was Benjamin *Templar's* father? *Nicky's* Ben, her son's best friend at kindergarten? Or they had been best friends, before the tragedy that had struck both boys at the end of November, plucking them asunder, and uncovering the shocking revelations that had torn Mardi's own world apart. They might have torn her heart apart, too, if her husband hadn't already crushed any remaining feeling she'd had for him, wearing it away in subtle, soul-destroying ways over the months leading up to his death.

Before either had a chance to say any more, Scoots burst up the steps onto the veranda ahead of Nicky, the powerful dog hurling himself at the stranger on his doorstep. But he wasn't growling or snarling—oh, no, not Scoots. His tail was thrashing to and fro like a scythe as his great paws landed on Cain Templar's shoulders, his moist pink tongue flicking deep wet kisses all over the man's startled face.

Looking more exasperated than angry, the man frowned and stepped back. "Okay, okay, you can get down now!"

he rapped, a command that had no effect whatsoever on Scoots.

Mardi, on a wicked impulse, didn't immediately come to the man's rescue. "You don't like dogs?" she asked sweetly, wondering if he was like her husband, Darrell, who'd only tolerated Scoots for Nicky's sake.

"Well-*behaved* dogs," he growled, trying to dodge Scoot's flashing tongue. "Well-*trained* dogs. You've never thought of taking this undisciplined pooch to a training school?"

Mardi's chin rose, her eyes glinting at the criticism. "I trained Scoots myself. He'll settle down in a minute. He's just checking you out." She paused, adding in some surprise, "He must like you. He doesn't jump up on everybody. He'd be growling if he didn't like you."

Cain Templar looked as if he'd prefer to be growled at than jumped on with dirty paws and a slobbering tongue.

Taking pity on him, Mardi belatedly pulled Scoots back away from him with a mildly scolding, "Down, Scoots, that's enough! Nicky, take him round the back, will you, before he wrecks the gentleman's fine suit." She was careful not to mention her visitor's name. "And shut the side gate after you."

She felt a certain wicked satisfaction at the thought of Cain Templar's suit being ruined. Maybe because it reminded her of Darrell's expensive designer suits and his other wild extravagances. Extravagances that had left his widow and young son penniless and in crushing debt.

"I'm sure it will survive," Cain Templar said dryly, brushing himself off.

And I'm sure you could afford to buy another one if it didn't, Mardi reflected, and paused to wonder if he actually *could* afford to buy his fine Italian suits, or if he was another Darrell, living well beyond his means.

Of course he wasn't. He was Cain Templar, the genuinely wealthy, highly successful merchant banker, whose glamorous wife, Sylvia, had been having an affair with her husband. And the Templars' home, which Darrell, her insatiably ambitious, social-climbing lawyer husband, had visited often and gone into raptures about, but which she had never seen or been invited to, was a magnificent harborside mansion in one of Sydney's most exclusive suburbs.

She turned away, watching Nicky and Scoots until they disappeared round the side of the house. How insensitive of this man to come here. His wife had ruined her life—ruined her *son's* life!

Mardi glowered. If only she hadn't fallen sick with the flu last September! Darrell had first met Sylvia Templar on the very morning he'd driven Nicky to kindergarten for the first time. Sylvia's husband, she recalled Darrell mentioning at the time, had just left on a two-month overseas business trip. How convenient *that* had turned out to be!

From the moment he met her, Darrell had openly raved about "Benjamin's beautiful mother," and how she was the perfect corporate wife...an asset to her husband and a real help to his career as a merchant banker. "She's an example to other wives," he'd enthused in his typically insensitive fashion. "Always impeccably groomed, beautifully dressed, the perfect hostess, at ease in any company... And she knows everybody—everybody who matters, that is. You could learn a lot from her."

Yeah...like how to play around with other women's husbands.

Darrell had relentlessly encouraged his son's friendship with Sylvia's five-year-old son, Ben, inviting Benjamin to their home at weekends and allowing Nicky to visit *their* home in return.

Mardi had tried, for her son's sake, to be friendly with Sylvia on the few occasions they'd met, either when Benjamin came to play, or on the rare evenings Darrell invited Sylvia to their home for a dinner party, along with Darrell's successful, influential friends and business colleagues. But usually he'd preferred to dine out. Without his wife.

How naive and unsuspecting she'd been! Even when Darrell started giving Sylvia Templar so-called "legal advice," which meant he had to see her more often still, for lunches or intimate dinners for two, or to attend Sylvia's fund-raising events, Mardi still didn't suspect—or she'd tried not to. She loathed jealousy and suspicion in wives, and with Sylvia's husband away, it was understandable— or so she managed to convince herself—that Darrell, as the woman's lawyer, would want to keep a close eye on her.

Looking back, it was painfully obvious that Darrell had fallen hook, line and sinker for Sylvia Templar's glossy wealth, glamour and impeccable social connections—to say nothing of her luxurious home and lifestyle.

Mardi had been so gullible! She still had no idea when Darrell's so-called "innocent relationship" with the beautiful Sylvia had changed into a fully fledged affair. She only knew that on the last Sunday in November, a couple of months after the two met, her husband and Cain Templar's wife had died together in a car crash in the Blue Mountains on a night when Darrell was supposedly returning from a law-ethics weekend conference in the mountains.

The gleaming BMW that Darrell had bought only two months earlier, courtesy of a hefty bank loan, had been wrecked beyond repair.

Neither Mardi nor Benjamin Templar's father had sent their sons back to the kindergarten for the final week of the term, or made any attempt to bring the boys together during the long summer break. Mardi, for her part, had wanted nothing more to do with the Templar family.

She'd assumed that Cain Templar had felt a similar disdain for her family. Maybe he'd *wanted* to keep away from them, but his son had finally worn him down, just as Nicky had been trying to do to her.

But to bring the boys together again now would be a ghastly mistake! She'd be moving away very soon, so why make it even more difficult for Nicky? For both boys?

Reluctantly she turned back. "You say you're here because of Benjamin," she said cautiously, frowning up at him.

"That's right. My son—" He stopped, his head jerking toward the open window at the front of the house. "Can you smell something burning?"

"Oh, heck!" She spun round. "My *cake!* My *pie!*"

Chapter Two

Mardi groaned as she dumped the charred remains of her pie and cake on the sink. Tonight's dinner ruined! She couldn't *afford* disasters like this.

She rushed to the window and opened it, then began fanning the air with a tea towel.

"This is my fault," Cain Templar apologized from behind, and she swung round, not realizing that he'd followed her to the kitchen.

"Well, yes, it is," she agreed, in no mood for her usual politeness. *What was she going to do about tonight's dinner?* "But there's nothing much you can do about it." She turned back to the sink. The pie was completely shriveled and dried out, but maybe she could cut off the charred edges of the cake and examine it to find out if the interior was still edible.

But she certainly wasn't going to try that in front of Cain Templar! It would look ridiculously penny-pinching to someone with his millions. If it happened to him, he'd simply go out and buy another pie and another cake. At one time, she might have, too.

"Oh, there must be something I can do," Cain said smoothly. "Look, I promised to take Benjamin to Mc-Donald's tonight..." He grimaced. "Not my own cup of tea, but he's been nagging me for a burger for ages and I couldn't keep fobbing him off and saying no. Why don't you and your son join us?" he invited, though there was little emotion in his voice, as if he had no more wish to see more of the Sinclairs than Mardi did of the Templars.

"Ben talks about Nicky incessantly," he added as she started to shake her head. "I gather they were close mates at kindergarten last term."

Mardi sighed. "Yes, they were," she said, stressing the past tense. "And thanks, Mr. Templar, but—"

"Cain," he murmured coolly.

"Cain. Thanks, but there's no need for you to take pity on us. It's my own fault for not removing the pie and the cake from the oven earlier. And I really don't think—" She stopped, waving a helpless hand. "Look, we can't talk in here." The smoke-filled air and the charred smell were making it impossible. "Let's move to the front of the house."

Nicky, hopefully, would stay out in the garden with Scoots until Cain Templar had gone. He need never know that the man who'd called had been his friend Ben's father.

As they turned to leave the kitchen, her grandfather hobbled in, a gnarled hand curled round his walking stick.

"What's burning?" he demanded in his thin, wavery voice.

"It's just the pie and cake I was baking, Grandpa." *Just?* She saw Grandpa frowning up at the tall dark man at her side and remembered her manners. "Oh...this is Cain Templar, Grandpa. He's here to discuss a—a business matter."

Her eyes warned her visitor not to dispute her statement. She didn't want Grandpa rushing out and blabbing to Nicky that the father of his beloved Ben was here.

With luck, Grandpa, who was getting a bit hard of hearing, wouldn't have caught the name "Templar" or made the connection with Sylvia Templar—*that Jezebel,* as he called her. It would be too embarrassing if he launched into a savage tirade on man-hungry wives who ran off with other women's husbands.

"My grandfather...Ernie Williams." She was edging toward the passage as she spoke.

"How do you do, sir?" Cain started to extend a hand, and then, as if fearing the old man would let go of his stick and topple over, let it drop, giving a brief nod instead.

The old man gave a cackle of laughter. "Long time since anybody called me 'sir.' Doesn't feel right. Call me Ernie."

"Right. Ernie."

Mardi sensed that Cain, well mannered as he was, would have no wish to hang around making polite conversation with her aging relative. Just as she had no wish to keep him here. "Grandpa," she said gently, "would you mind running Nicky's bath and calling him inside when it's ready? And *please* be careful in the bathroom," she warned. The last thing she needed was for Grandpa to fall and do even worse damage to his hip.

"Sure, love." She felt his squinting gaze lingering on them as she ushered Cain Templar away. Grandpa still felt protective of her, as he'd been for most of her life. And since Darrell's betrayal, he'd eyed all smart-suited businessmen with mistrust—though Cain Templar's polite charm seemed to have disarmed him, at least for the time being.

She led Cain to the front lounge room and waved him in. The room was attractively furnished—Darrell had made sure of that—but the furniture didn't belong to her, she'd discovered after the funeral, any more than the house did. Unknown to her, Darrell had never paid for any of it, and now the house and the new furniture were being repossessed.

The walls and shelves had already been stripped of the expensive oil paintings and decorative ornaments Darrell had insisted on buying—another sore subject—though she'd sold them for far less than he'd paid for them. Some *hadn't* been paid for, and she'd been faced with the bill.

She didn't invite Cain to sit down. That would be making him too welcome. "I don't think it would be a good idea for Nicky and Ben to see each other again," she said without preamble. "We'll be leaving here in a couple of weeks—sooner, if I can find another place before then. Our house is already sold...." But the money had gone to the bank, not to her.

Cain narrowed his eyes as he looked down at her for a disconcertingly long moment. "Too many bitter memories?" he asked finally, a hint of his own bitterness evident in the twist of his mouth.

She shrugged. Let him think that was why she was selling up and moving away. It was close enough to the truth. The house *did* have bitter memories. Especially the queen-size bed in the main bedroom. Darrell had stopped making love to her about the time he'd started seeing Sylvia Templar. He'd made excuses about having to work late, or having to entertain business clients until late, pleading tiredness when he came to bed, if she happened to be still awake.

At first he'd made token apologies for leaving her alone so often, insisting he was doing it all for *her*—for her and Nicky. But as the weeks went on, he'd stopped seeming to care, becoming irritable and touchy, and finding fault with everything she did.

When he'd started comparing her openly with Sylvia Templar, she'd finally lost her patience—and her temper.

"If she's so perfect, why don't you go and live with *her*?"

He'd thrown up his hands in disgust. "Heaven help me, Mardi, sometimes I wish I could. At least she and I are on the same wavelength!"

Mardi had felt a coldness brush down her spine, the unpalatable truth hitting her—her husband had fallen in love with Sylvia Templar! Or with what she represented. Wealth, luxury, the best connections. "So I'm not good enough for you anymore?" she'd flung back, her self-esteem at an all-time low.

"Oh, for pity's sake, Mardi, don't be so *suburban*. You're becoming such a nag and a bore. I don't need these kind of hassles. I need a wife who'll support me, not pull me down and hold me back."

She felt as if he'd struck her. "When have I ever pulled you down or tried to hold you back? I've let you do whatever you want to make a success of your life. I've looked after the house and the garden, I've raised Nicky practically single-handedly, I've made most of our own clothes and I've taken on a part-time job to make ends meet. All this to give *you* the time and the space to become the successful lawyer you want to be."

"You ungrateful witch! If it wasn't for Nicky—" He'd stopped abruptly, glowering at her. "Oh, hell, I'm going out! A man can't come home for peace and quiet anymore."

It was two weeks later that he'd gone to the Blue Mountains for the so-called legal-ethics conference he'd never returned from, and amid the shock of his death, and the death of his female passenger, the truth of his double life had come out.

Bitter memories? Yes…she still felt bitter that her husband had left his family so badly in debt, and equally bitter—more bitter than heartbroken—about his affair with Sylvia Templar. But she also wondered if she could have been partly at fault herself, as Darrell had accused her. Had she driven him into Sylvia's arms through not being supportive enough, not wanting the kind of high-flying life he'd wanted, not attending more social functions with him? But he hadn't *wanted* her to. She hadn't fit in, hadn't "played the game." The truth was, she hadn't felt comfortable with his shallow, social-climbing, money-mad friends. They'd left her cold.

Maybe she should have tried harder to keep up with him. Her lip curled at the thought. *To live beyond her means, as he'd lived beyond his? To lie and cheat and fool people into believing she was richer and more important than she was? To fawn on people she despised?* No, she thought, recoiling. She would have been *lowering* herself, not lifting herself to her husband's level. She would have been as bad as he was, as dishonest, as shallow. She refused to feel guilty about the way she'd handled her life.

But her confidence had been battered, as well as her trust in men. In husbands. In love. It would be a long time before she would ever trust another man. Or feel confident enough in *herself* to take the risk of trusting another man.

Her eyes clouded. How would she ever find peace of mind until her husband's massive debts were paid off… until Nicky had his infected tonsils removed and was fit and healthy again…until Grandpa's painful hip was replaced?

Cain Templar watched the changing expressions in Mardi's long-lashed amber eyes and wondered if it was repressed anger he was seeing, or a deeply buried pain and heartbreak. It was hard to tell.

She was a surprise to him. He'd been half expecting Darrell Sinclair's widow to be a mousy little thing with a whining voice and little personality—a downtrodden, wishy-washy woman who'd been completely under her unfaithful husband's thumb. But there was a natural warmth and vibrancy about her, a spontaneous spring in her step, which even her husband's betrayal and the shock of his death hadn't managed to quench.

And he'd seen her before, he realized. He'd bumped into her at Ben's kindergarten last September, on the morning he'd left for New York. He'd had no idea who she was then, or that the boy with her was Ben's friend Nicky. Normally his wife or a babysitter had driven Ben to and from kindergarten each day, but on that particular day he'd had a late-morning plane to catch and had taken Ben to St. Mark's himself.

He'd barely glanced at the woman at the gate—an ordinary, unremarkable woman, he'd thought in that first fleeting glimpse. And then his gaze had collided with hers, and the unusual amber color of her eyes, beneath her long golden lashes, had caught his attention for an unsettling instant, the morning sunlight turning her eyes to pure gold. Her soft brown hair, pulled back in a neat ponytail—far neater than it was now—had caught the sun, too, and gleamed with honeyed highlights.

Little did he know then that their lives would become entwined a few months later in the most bitter of ways. *Her* husband…and *his* wife. His chest heaved. And their sons, by a cruel twist of fate, were best friends.

Which was why he was here now. The *only* reason he was here, he reminded himself sharply.

"As I said, I'm here because of Benjamin, my son." Cain's voice was harsher than he'd intended it to be. He felt oddly off balance, struck again by the steady warmth of those unusual amber eyes, regarding him unblinkingly through wayward honeyed strands from her loosening ponytail.

Annoyed at his reaction, he flicked his gaze away, letting it sweep down her flour-smudged T-shirt to her equally grubby shorts, which looked as if she'd wiped her floury hands on them.

"My son's becoming uncontrollable," he admitted grimly, trying not to look at the long, lightly tanned legs below the short shorts. Disgusted with himself for even noticing them, he snapped his gaze away from her altogether, to stare at the wall behind. *What was it about this ordinary suburban housewife that was causing this edginess in him?*

"Ben's very moody," he muttered, dragging his thoughts back to his son. "He won't do as he's told, he has temper tantrums like a two-year-old and he's been through at least five baby-sitters since my—since Christmas."

Five baby-sitters? Mardi felt a rush of compassion for the small boy who'd lost his mother and been left with strangers since. Why hadn't his *father* taken time off work and cared for the boy himself during the long summer holidays?

"I've tried everything," Cain Templar growled. "I've even taken odd days off myself, when an incompetent baby-sitter has let me down."

Odd days off... How magnanimous of him, Mardi thought in scorn. Obviously today wasn't one of those odd days. She glared at his immaculate business suit and tie, guessing that he'd come here straight from his office. No rushing home to his son first....

"Where is Ben now?" she asked, feeling for the boy.

"He's with a new baby-sitter." Cain grimaced. "I've

spoken to Ben on the phone and he says he hates her already. I had to dangle the bait of McDonald's to calm him down." He shook his head. "It's not as if he's had nothing to do during the holidays. He's been to playgrounds and kids' movies and the beach, and I've arranged for our friends' children to come and play with him, but he doesn't seem to care about anything or anyone." His mouth tightened. "Anyone except—"

"He's just lost his mother!" Mardi cried, wanting to forestall what she guessed he was about to say. *Anyone except his friend Nicky.* Ben, she thought regretfully, would have to forget Nicky.

Cain Templar's blue eyes grew remote, unreadable, at the mention of Ben's mother. "It's been weeks now. He's getting worse, not better."

"The long summer holidays can drag for a small child. He should be okay once he starts school." *Only, he won't find Nicky there.* "There's only another week to go," she said brightly.

"It's not his mother or St. Mark's that Ben's missing," Cain said flatly.

Mardi held her breath, at a loss to know how to stop what she knew was coming. "It's his friend Nicky. Your son, Nicky. Ben keeps asking if he can play with him. I've tried every diversion I can think of. I was sure you wouldn't want to encourage their friendship any more than I do."

She shook her head vigorously. At least they agreed on that!

His chest swelled in a sigh. "But keeping Ben away from Nicky hasn't worked. It's just made him more rebellious and difficult. I don't know if Nicky's been missing Ben, too...."

His eyes pierced hers and she found herself floundering. How could she deny it? "Mmm..."

He looked satisfied. "Well, the only solution, as I see it, is to let them play together and hope they'll get sick of each other before long, as young children do."

She swallowed. "And if they don't?"

He drew in his lips. "Once they're both back at St. Mark's, with other children around, they'll make other friends."

She took a deep breath. "Nicky won't be going back to St. Mark's this year."

His eyebrows shot up. "Why not? Even if you move out of the area, you'll still want to send your son to St. Mark's, won't you, where he'll be with children he knows? It would be a shame not to go back...it's a very good school."

Very good, and very expensive, Mardi thought, but as she began to shake her head, Cain gave a wry smile.

"Keep them apart and they'll only go on pining for each other."

She puffed out a sigh. Heck, Cain Templar was persistent. "Throw them back together and they're more likely to get *closer* to each other, if I know Nicky." Nicky was loyal to a fault. "Look, it's best if they don't see each other at all. Nicky won't be going back to St. Mark's, so there's really no more to be said."

"But why *not,* for pity's sake? You haven't even found another place to live yet. Why not send him back until you do?"

"Because I can't aff—" She stopped, on the brink of blurting out the shameful truth.

He frowned. "Can't *afford* it?" The expression in his eyes changed. Hardening, rather than softening. "Are you saying that your husband didn't leave you and your family sufficiently provided for? I thought he was a successful lawyer." He glanced round at the expensive furnishings, the new carpet, the impressive built-in shelves lining an entire wall.

She spread her hands helplessly. "He had…a lot of expenses. Overwhelming expenses." She wasn't going to run down Nicky's father…not now that Darrell was gone and unable to harm them any further. She was determined to keep his image as a loving, caring father intact for his son's sake. "Please… I don't want to talk about it."

Cain regarded her speculatively. She must have loved the creep…and must love him still, despite the bitterness and hurt he'd inflicted on her. Poor woman. And it was *his* wife who'd taken Mardi's husband from her, *his* wife who was responsible for her pain. In some odd way, it made him feel responsible, too.

"Look…whether you send Nicky back to St. Mark's or not, the boys can still see each other…if you'll let them," he argued on his son's behalf, though in his heart he didn't want the boys thrown back together any more than she did. Seeing more of the Sinclair family—of Darrell Sinclair's widow in particular—would be a constant and humiliating reminder of their spouses' shoddy affair.

But what *he* thought or felt or wanted didn't matter. It was Ben who mattered…the son he'd taken little notice of in the past five years. The ruthless quest for wealth, success and position—and damn it, for parental approval, too—had taken over his life, coming close to alienating him from his son. Ironic, when he thought about it. He'd been so determined that history wouldn't repeat itself.

Mardi saw his mouth tighten and felt a shiver brush down her spine. Cain Templar would be a dangerous man to get mixed up with.

"Doesn't Ben have any grandparents who can help out?" As the question left her lips, her eyes grew pensive. Nicky had never known any of his grandparents, only his great-grandfather Ernie. Her parents had died when she was six, and Darrell's widowed father, who'd been in a nursing home for years, unable to recognize anyone, had died early last year.

"No." A cold, unequivocal *no*. "Sylvia had no parents, and my father and stepmother live in New Zealand." A sudden chill turned his blue eyes to ice. "We're not close."

Mardi's gaze searched his. Was there pain under the ice? Anger? It was impossible to tell. She shivered again, the coldness in his eyes seeming to chill the very air around her.

"You didn't get on with your stepmother?" she ventured, injecting sympathy into her voice, hoping it might make him reveal a bit more about himself.

"I didn't get on with my *father*." His face was granite hard, his frosty eyes clearly warning her *Subject closed.*

She backed off. "I didn't realize you were a New Zealander," she said lightly. She would never have picked it from his accent, which sounded more Australian, or even slightly English.

"I'm not. I'm a naturalized Australian."

"But you were born and brought up in New Zealand?"

"I left when I was eighteen, to go to Sydney University." His eyes grew remote again, and even more discouraging.

But this time she didn't take the hint. "And you haven't been back since then?"

She almost took a step back as his powerful frame tensed, his face darkening. "Once," he ground out at length. "When Ben was about eighteen months old." He'd thought, more fool he, that the sight of his first grandchild might have softened his father's stony heart, but it hadn't— any more than his own growing wealth and success had impressed his narrow-minded parent.

Mardi swiftly brought the conversation back to Ben. "Well, what about aunts and uncles? Do you have any brothers or sisters who could help you with Ben? Or cousins who could play with him?"

"No." As sharp and implacable as before. "I have a couple of stepsiblings, but as far as they're concerned, I don't exist. And vice versa," he said with grim satisfaction, crushing any pity she might have had for him.

"Look..." His tone changed, the grimness wiped out as if it had never been. "Our two boys still have a week before school starts," he reminded her. "If we allow the boys to see each other, a week should be long enough, hopefully, for them to get over their obsession with each other...and calm Ben down a bit."

Mardi shook her head doubtfully. "I still don't think it's a good idea...."

His brow lowered again. "You're being very hard on the boys. I thought you'd have more compassion." A hard, silvery glint kindled in his blue eyes. He looked almost threatening for a second. A man, Mardi thought unsteadily, not used to losing his battles...and not liking it when he did.

"So what if they do get closer?" Cain threw out the challenge. "If it helps my son—and he badly needs help—it's worth taking that risk." A betraying roughness edged his voice.

It was the first real emotion he'd shown and it pierced her own fragile armor. Especially his accusation that she didn't feel for the boys.

She tilted her chin. "I *am* thinking of the boys. They've been apart since before kindergarten broke up last year. Why throw them back together now, when we know it will only be for a short time?" Why throw the two of *us* together, she wanted to add, when it will only keep the bitter memories alive for both of us?

But Mardi knew in her heart that it wasn't bitter memories she was worried about. It had more to do with a tall, handsome, potently attractive man with cobalt-blue eyes who'd been haunting her dreams for months. Why did that stranger at the gate have to turn out to be Sylvia Templar's husband and Benjamin Templar's father? And why did he have to turn up here, making demands that would force her to see more of him?

"They're only five years old," he said, visibly changing tack, the hard light in his eye softening a trifle. "They don't understand what's happened, or why they're being kept apart. They only know they want to see each other again."

He leaned forward, using the full force of his compelling blue gaze. "I know it will be as difficult for you as it will for me, Mrs. Sinclair, but I think we should put our own feelings aside...for the sake of our sons."

For the sake of our sons. Mardi felt a tremor, recalling Nicky's plaintive pleas to see Ben again. *Was* she being selfish by keeping the boys apart? Was she thinking more of herself than two little boys in need? "Mardi," she reminded him absently, as she found herself wavering.

"Mardi." He gave a brief smile, and her eyes flickered under its impact. What, she wondered dazedly, would a real smile be like?

"Look, let the boys see each other...for as long as you're still here." Cain injected a note of pleading into his voice. "Come to dinner with us tonight. A casual meal together to break the ice."

She thought of Nicky's unhappy face, of his constant pleas to see Ben, and felt herself weakening even more. But she wasn't going to cave in yet. "We—we can't come tonight. There's my grandfather to—"

"Maybe he'd enjoy it, too."

She shook her head, her eyes wistful. "I don't think so. He doesn't go out much. He has a bad hip and it's too painful for him. He's—" She was about to say "waiting for an operation," but Cain Templar wouldn't understand why anyone should have to wait. He'd have private health insurance and wouldn't even know about waiting lists at public hospitals.

"Besides," she continued, "Grandpa doesn't eat much these days." Which was just as well, with tonight's dinner lying in ruins. She still had some vegetable soup she'd made a couple of days ago, she remembered. She could add some potatoes—she had one or two left. And she had bread in the freezer. That would have to do for tonight. Followed by whatever she could salvage of her carrot cake.

Cain thrust his face closer, and she felt her breath stop for a disturbing second. "Then let Nicky come and play with Ben tomorrow. At our home. It's Saturday and I'll be home all day." He pinned her with his magnetic blue gaze. "I'll come and pick him up in the morning, give the boys lunch and drop Nicky home again later in the day."

She hesitated, biting her lip. "I—I'd prefer to have the boys here—" she faltered "—where I can keep an eye on them myself. I—I like to know exactly where Nicky is and what he's doing." She wasn't sure she trusted Cain Templar. He obviously wasn't used to looking after small boys. What if Nicky fell over and broke his glasses and no one was there to help him? What if Ben had a temper tantrum and Nicky couldn't deal with it?

Cain looked faintly surprised, which didn't unduly surprise *her*. He and his wife, she was well aware, had been in the habit of leaving their son with baby-sitters—though Sylvia had shown more interest in Ben, she reflected caustically, when she'd started her involvement with Darrell.

Their sons, wanting to play with each other after kinder-garten or at weekends, had given them a perfect cover, a perfect excuse to see each other.

Of course, they'd soon found an even more convincing excuse to see each other—*alone*. The lonely, neglected wife, needing legal advice from her new lawyer friend. Darrell had never told Mardi what *kind* of legal advice Sylvia Templar had sought.

Perhaps Sylvia Templar had been seeking a divorce from her husband and Darrell had been giving her advice, or even setting the wheels into motion.

Had she? Mardi's teeth clamped down on her lip. And had Darrell—besotted as he'd been with this rich, beautiful, perfect woman, whose home he'd described as a palace—been planning to divorce his *wife?* His boring suburban housewife?

Mardi jumped as she felt Cain Templar's hand on her arm. "I meant for you to come, too...naturally," he said, his voice gentler than she'd heard it so far. But his eyes were unreadable, projecting little warmth. Well, perhaps hers weren't, either, she thought wryly. They were, after all, arranging this reunion purely for the sake of their sons.

"Ah..." was all she could say, the last of her arguments crumbling.

"How about I pick you both up at ten-thirty?" he suggested, a gleam of satisfaction in his eyes. "Is that too early?"

"No...ten-thirty's fine," she said faintly, wondering what she was getting herself into. To spend a whole day with Cain Templar... How unwise was *that?* And why would he want to spend his time with *her?* Simply because she'd insisted on being there to watch over her son?

Her eyes flickered in quick suspicion.

"If I'm coming, too, there's no need for you to come

and pick us up," she said firmly. "I have my own car."
She could always park it a few doors down the street so
that Cain Templar wouldn't be embarrassed by her old
bomb. Darrell had bought her a secondhand car under suf-
ferance, when she'd insisted on going back to work part-
time. Her husband hadn't believed in working wives. Wives
were meant to stay at home and run the household. In return
for his "generosity," she'd had to agree to the purchase of
his ill-fated BMW.

"As you wish." Cain's blue eyes were as cool as his
tone. "Well, I must go," he said, and she nodded, pleased
that he seemed anxious, finally, to get home to his son.

Next minute he was gone, leaving the air crackling and
swirling in his wake. She had to take several deep breaths
on her way to the bathroom. Cain Templar was a forceful,
dynamic presence and an incredibly persuasive man. Determined as she'd been not to get involved with the Templar family, he'd swept all her arguments aside.

But his motives weren't so clear. Did he genuinely love
and care about his son—the son he'd left recently for eight
long weeks? The son he'd left so often with baby-sitters?
Or did he simply want a more controllable son and a more
peaceful, undemanding life at home?

She sighed as she trudged back along the passage.

About twenty minutes later, as she was drying Nicky's
hair after his bath, she heard the front doorbell ring again.

"Oh, no," she groaned. "Who is it *now?*"

"I'll get it," Grandpa shouted from the den, and she
heard his stick tap-tapping along the passage.

"Well, be careful," she yelled out. "Take it slowly."
Grandpa tried so hard to help her, but every movement was
painful for him, every step a hazard.

"I am, I am!"

A few moments later she heard voices, and footsteps

coming along the passage to the kitchen. One was Grandpa's voice and the other a deeper voice that sounded suspiciously like—

Her hands froze midair.

"Mummy, you've stopped rubbing!"

"Sorry." She resumed her rubbing, but with her ears pricked, trying to pick out what the two men in the kitchen were saying. Why had Cain Templar come back? Had he left something behind? Or had he already changed his mind about tomorrow? Maybe he'd remembered something more important he had to do.

Mardi tightened her lips, wondering if he was in the habit of letting his son down. She just hoped he hadn't told Ben in advance that he intended to visit Nicky.

She frowned, straining to hear. She could only hear Grandpa's voice now, and she would have sworn he was *thanking* the other man for something. But for what? Had Cain told him about tomorrow's planned reunion for the two boys? Grandpa knew how much Nicky wanted to see Ben again. But would he be thanking Cain for bringing *that Jezebel's* son back into their lives?

She heard her grandfather calling out goodbye with a gusto she hadn't heard from him for some time, then firm footsteps—not Grandpa's—sounded again in the passage and a moment later the front door slammed shut. Cain Templar had gone.

She released the breath she hadn't realized she'd been holding. Well, he obviously hadn't come back to see *her*. She wasn't sure if she felt disappointment or relief.

She heard the tap-tap of Grandpa's stick coming from the kitchen, and a moment later his head poked round the bathroom door. "That was your friend again. He brought us dinner."

"He brought us *what?*"

"He said it was his fault you burned our dinner, and he's brought us another pie and another cake, from some home-made cake shop, he said."

Mardi rose slowly to her feet, touched, despite herself, by Cain's thoughtful gesture. Or was it more that he felt sorry for her, because he'd guessed that she was hurting financially? She flushed, glad that she hadn't had the embarrassment of having to accept his offer herself. She didn't want anyone's charity! Especially not his.

"Wow! Let's go and look!" Nicky made a dash for the kitchen, with Grandpa, broadly smiling, hobbling behind. Mardi didn't follow immediately, cleaning the tub and tidying up first. But despite her misgivings about accepting charity from a virtual stranger—from a *Templar*—it was a load off her mind to have another pie and cake to give to her family for dinner.

She hadn't had too many loads taken off her mind lately.

Chapter Three

"Are we nearly there, Mummy?"

"Nearly, darling." Mardi glanced over her shoulder at her fidgety, bright-eyed son and smiled. If she'd had any doubts about accepting Cain Templar's invitation to his home today, the glow on Nicky's face since she'd told him he'd be seeing Ben again had chased them away. If there were to be any consequences in the future, she would worry about them then. "Here's Ben's street now."

"Yippee!" Nicky strained forward. "I see it! It's the house with the high wall." He'd been here before, of course. With his father.

Mardi slowed down. "I think I'll park here in the shade of this tree. We can walk from here." Not that anyone behind that long high wall would be able to see her car, wherever she parked it.

Nicky undid his seat belt and jumped out the second she pulled up. "Come on, Mummy. I want to see Ben."

Mardi was anxious to see Ben, too. She just hoped that Nicky's presence would have a calming effect on the troubled boy and that Ben's tantrums and uncontrollable behavior wouldn't rub off on her son. She had enough problems!

One was the thought of seeing Cain Templar again. *I don't want this any more than you do,* he'd said, stressing that his invitation was purely for his son's sake. He didn't want *her* there, as well, but she'd given him little choice. And she didn't regret the stand she'd taken, little as *she'd* wanted to come herself. There was no way she was going to dump Nicky on Cain Templar's doorstep and just leave him there—no matter how grand his home was or how lofty his standing might be in the community. She didn't know or particularly like the man, and she had no idea if she could trust him to look after her son, let alone cope with two lively five-year-olds.

Oh, Mardi, who are you kidding? She sighed, knowing she had a deeper, more shameful reason for not wanting to come today. What if he could read the embarrassing truth in her eyes? The truth that she subconsciously lusted after him.

Subconsciously... That was the key word. She stuck out her jaw. *Consciously,* she would no more want to get tied up with him than with...than with another Darrell Sinclair.

When they reached the Templars' gate—a solid timber gate as high as the wall—she paused to take a breath and collect herself. She was wearing her best tailored slacks and a neat white blouse, with a tote bag slung over her shoulder. Somehow her old faded jeans and a T-shirt hadn't seemed right for a visit to the Templars' luxurious home.

She saw a security intercom beside the gate and pressed a button. A woman with a foreign accent answered, brusquely telling her to come in and to proceed to the front door of the house. Mardi assumed she must be a maid or a housekeeper. *Or Ben's latest baby-sitter?* The woman didn't sound young enough, or refined enough, to be a special woman friend of the lofty Cain Templar.

The thought that he might have a woman friend brought a frown to Mardi's brow and an unaccountable twinge, which annoyed her so intensely that her thoughts turned vicious. She wondered if he'd had a mistress while Sylvia was still alive, and if the humiliation had driven his wife into the arms of another man—Mardi Sinclair's ruthlessly ambitious husband!

Mardi shook the thought from her mind and pushed the gate open, ushering Nicky through.

Her eyes widened as she saw Cain Templar's home. She knew that the house faced the harbor down below, but even from the back, the massive white-walled double-story mansion was a sight to behold.

There was a lock-up garage and what looked like a guest house to one side, and a paved terrace and neat garden beds between the street wall and the house. A row of Italian stone urns, spilling over with brightly colored flowers, led to a covered porch.

The door suddenly burst open and a small boy hurtled through. Mardi recognized him immediately as Ben. Tall, dark-haired and blue-eyed, he was a miniature version of his father—but with noticeably more warmth and enthusiasm.

"Hi, Nicky!" Ben cried out as he spied his long-lost friend.

A smile lit up Nicky's small face as he broke free of his mother and darted forward. "Hi, Ben."

Not a trace of shyness from either boy, Mardi noted with a faint mistiness in her eye as Ben grabbed Nicky by the hand and dragged him inside. A swarthy, middle-aged woman with no trace of a welcoming smile was standing by the door, but she stepped aside as the boys burst past her.

"I apologize for my—" Mardi began, but the woman had already turned on her heel.

"Follow me," she said, without pausing to introduce herself.

Mardi found herself in a spacious circular reception hall, with a sweeping staircase that brought *Gone with the Wind* to mind. Above her was the largest, most impressive crystal chandelier that she'd ever seen.

The boys, their shoes clattering on the gleaming, marble-tiled floor, were fast disappearing along an unbelievably wide, seemingly endless central passage, heading for the harbor-facing front.

So much marble, Mardi noted in wonder. Italian, for sure. She wondered what her young son thought of all this magnificence. He probably hadn't even noticed. He'd only be interested in Ben. And of course, he'd been here before, with his father.

"Come!" The poker-faced housekeeper was already flip-flopping after the boys in her flat-heeled scuffs. Mardi quickened her steps, half expecting Cain to appear from one of the exquisitely furnished rooms that she spied at intervals on her way to the front door—all of them, she noted in bemusement, following the same basic white theme. Beautiful, but hopelessly impractical. She wondered how anyone could possibly keep the place clean with an exuberant young boy in the house.

Poor Ben. *She'd* have tantrums, too, Mardi decided, if she had to live in such pristine perfection!

Where *was* Ben's father? she pondered when Cain Templar failed to appear from any of the rooms. The boys had vanished from sight. When the housekeeper ushered her through the impressive glass doors at the front of the house and led her out onto a broad, balustraded terrace, she assumed that Cain had ordered his maid to get his guests out of his house at the earliest possible opportunity.

In front of her stood a white outdoor table with a set of matching chairs, set with drinking glasses and bowls of nuts and cookies.

Her gaze swept past them. "Wow!" She blinked against the sunlight as a breathtaking vista opened up in front of her.

Wide stone steps led down to a beautifully landscaped garden on several levels, with exotic plants, elegant statues and sweeping lawns—in fact, the two boys were already chasing each other round one of the lawns, among the statues, as she watched. A kidney-shape swimming pool lay to one side, with, she was relieved to see, a discreet iron-railing safety fence all round. On a lower level was an immaculately kept grass tennis court. Beyond lay the harbor in all its glory, with white-sailed yachts and other craft skimming across the shimmering blue water, and in the distance she spied the familiar outline of the Sydney Harbor Bridge.

She swallowed. What a view! She hoped Cain appreciated it. She glanced back at his house. With its soaring white columns rising to the upper-story balcony, it looked even grander and more magnificent from the front.

Mardi felt her throat go dry. She'd known the Templars were wealthy—their money and lavish lifestyle were what had attracted her husband to the glamorous Sylvia in the first place—but she hadn't realized the extent of their wealth. This awesome property must be worth millions.

No wonder Darrell had been impressed. This was the kind of lifestyle her husband had longed for. His spending and debts had soared out of all control in his attempt to emulate it.

And she was paying for his folly. For his greed.

"Mr. Templar will be with you shortly," the housekeeper informed her, still without cracking a smile. Maybe, Mardi mused with a touch of cynicism, the Templars had forbidden their staff to smile or fraternize with their guests. "He had an important phone call," the woman added.

Business on a *Saturday?* Mardi shrugged. Why should she care? She'd be happier, and certainly a lot more relaxed, without him. "That's fine. I'll just stay here and watch over the boys."

But she wasn't destined to be happier and more relaxed, because in less than a minute Cain joined her, striding from the house with athletic ease and an unconsciously arrogant air of self-confidence.

She had to gulp a few times before he reached her. Having only seen him in an immaculate business suit and tie, seeing him now in a casual polo shirt and jeans—well, never in a million years would she have envisaged him in *jeans!* Yet he looked so *right* in them, so at ease in them. And so darned sexy!

How could Sylvia Templar ever have looked at another man, even during her husband's lengthy absences?

Mardi's thoughts darkened. The very fact that he *was* so sexy undoubtedly meant that he had women throwing themselves at him wherever he went. Maybe he hadn't been able to resist their advances, and his wife had grown tired of his roving ways and decided that what was good for the goose was equally as good for the gander.

Her mind kept coming back, she realized, to *his* affairs…*his* philandering…kept shifting blame to *him*. Why, she despaired, was she so determined to think the worst of *him*, when it was his glamorous *wife*, of her own free will, who had chased and stolen her husband?

Would she ever find out the real truth? Did she honestly *want* to?

"Mardi," Cain said, flashing her a mind-blowing smile. But *she* wasn't going to cave in under it, she vowed. Charm was only skin-deep, after all. Her husband, Darrell, had possessed charm in abundance. He could switch it on and off like a tap.

"Good morning, Cain." She kept her own smile cool. "If you're busy," she offered, "I can look after the boys. I'd be happy to."

"Where *are* they?" he asked, glancing round. He hadn't declined her offer, she noticed. She'd give him another minute or two—he'd stay that long out of politeness or a sense of obligation—and then he'd be off. "Ah..." He frowned. "*There* they are."

She followed his gaze, her heart sinking as she saw the two boys trying to climb the wire fence surrounding the tennis court. Oh, no, she thought. Now he'll think Nicky's a bad influence. And she was worried about *Ben's* bad behavior rubbing off on Nicky.

"They were playing chasey a moment ago," she said with a guilty flush. "I just took my eyes off them for a minute." To look at *you*—more fool me. "I'll run down and put a stop to it." She shot off before he could stop her—if he intended to.

"They won't be doing it for long," he called after her. "The wire will cut into their fingers."

She didn't even glance round as she flew down the steps. As soon as she was close enough for the boys to hear her, she shouted. "Get *down*, Nicky! You know better than to climb on other people's fences. And you must *never* climb a tennis court fence. You'll ruin it."

"You, too, Ben. I've warned you before."

Mardi jumped at the sound of Cain's voice, not realizing

he'd followed her. Both boys dropped to the ground, rubbing their smarting hands. "There's nothing else to climb here," Ben complained. "Nicky has big trees at his place."

Not for much longer, Mardi thought with a sigh. Their new place, if she ever found a suitable home for her brood, would be unlikely even to have a garden.

"Elena's bringing some drinks out onto the terrace for you," Cain told the boys. "Let's see who can get up there first."

The two boys shot off, and Mardi held her breath. Ben was much taller and faster than Nicky, and she was afraid that her son would try so hard to keep up with his lanky friend that he'd trip over and break his glasses.

"A race might tire them out," Cain commented hopefully, "and make them settle down a bit."

"They seem very happy to see each other," Mardi conceded, still watching anxiously as she and Cain headed off after the boys—at a more leisurely pace.

She only took her eyes off Nicky when he safely reached the terrace and flopped into an outdoor chair. Ben was already pouncing on the bowl of cookies, while Elena poured drinks for them from a big jug of orange juice.

Mardi glanced around. There was no doubt about it...it was a beautifully designed garden, with its slim ornamental pines and neat flower beds, its well-clipped lawns and graceful statues. Hardly a garden for boisterous little boys.

There were no trees suitable for climbing, as Ben had pointed out, no hardy shrubs for playing hide-and-seek, no playground equipment, no sandpit, no areas specifically set aside for energetic wear and tear. Cain Templar would probably throw a fit if his son tried to stick cricket stumps into his immaculate lawn or trampled on one of his exotic plants. Or worse, knocked over one of those slender statues dotting the lawn.

"Have you ever thought of buying a jungle gym or a swing for Ben?" she asked. "Boys love to climb. Well, you've just seen how they…" She trailed off as Cain's dark brow drew down in a frown. And no wonder, she thought in immediate self-reproach. She'd been here for five minutes and she was offering suggestions that in his eyes, no doubt, would desecrate the place!

"My wife believed that play equipment would spoil the view…as well as the aesthetics of the garden." Cain's impassive tone gave no clue to his own thoughts on the subject. "It was difficult enough persuading her to fence the pool. The garden was her pride and joy…. She oversaw everything that went into it."

Oversaw, Mardi noted. No, Sylvia Templar wouldn't have soiled her well-manicured hands by doing the gardening herself. But she *would* have employed the very best landscaping artists and gardeners.

"And she had to live with it more often than I did," Cain added with a shrug. "I've always worked long hours, including weekends, and I've spent a lot of my time away from home on business."

Leaving his wife at home alone…*feeling lonely and neglected?*

Mardi shrugged off her sour thoughts. She was supposed to be thinking of what was best for his *son.* She turned her mind back to swings and monkey bars.

So, it was Cain's *wife* who'd banned play equipment. But his wife was no longer here. Couldn't Cain put his son's needs first now?

"We do have a gymnasium under the house," Cain said. "There's all kinds of exercise equipment there."

Mardi pursed her lips. Exercise bikes and treadmills? Not quite the same as outdoor swings, slides and monkey bars…or a cubby house. Nicky was forever building cubby houses at home...out of old cartons, under drooping trees, in bushes. She couldn't imagine cardboard cartons being allowed to litter the Templars' impeccably kept yard. As for hanging ropes and a tire from a tree to make a swing, as she'd done for Nicky, there were no trees here big enough.

Her spirits dipped as she remembered that soon Nicky would have no rope swing, no trees to climb, no garden to build a cubby house in. Maybe not even room to play.

"But that's not what you mean, is it?" Cain's eyes were on her face. "You mean outdoor play equipment. Designed specially for kids."

She hesitated, then nodded. "You could put a swing or a slide around the side of the house somewhere, out of direct sight," she suggested boldly.

Cain jerked a shoulder. "There's a granny flat and a double garage on one side of the house, and a paved barbecue and entertaining area, with border shrubs, on the other. But I guess there'd be room there somewhere...."

Mardi's jaw dropped slightly. He was actually going to consider it?

Emboldened, she added, "And maybe you could move those statues in your lawn closer to the garden beds, to avoid them being knocked over when the boys run around."

"Mmmm...right. Any other ideas?" Cain asked as they climbed the steps to the terrace.

The faint dryness in his tone brought a tinge of pink to her cheeks. He'd sensed that she'd been less than impressed with his perfect garden. But she'd been looking at it purely from a child's point of view, from a practical point of view.

"I'm sorry." Her tone was placating. "You must think I'm extremely rude. I haven't even told you how beautiful your garden is."

The corner of his mouth tweaked. "I *know* how beautiful it is. What I need to know is how to make it more child-friendly. I'd appreciate your honest opinion—if you can think of anything else."

Cain caught the surprise in her eyes as she glanced up at him, and in the same instant the sun picked up the rare amber of her eyes and made them glow like molten gold. He felt something stir, deep in his gut. *Lust...* What else? Cynicism twisted his lips. He'd fallen in *lust* with another pair of eyes once.... Sylvia's eyes had been just as beautiful...not golden, but a dramatic, depthless black.

He scowled. He didn't want to equate this woman with his wife. Mardi, he sensed, was a different kettle of fish altogether. From what he'd observed so far, her values and priorities would be totally different from Sylvia's. She cared about her son...cared about her grandfather...cared about people other than herself. And she wouldn't be the kind of woman, he suspected, who would play around behind her husband's back...or, for that matter, be the kind of woman *he* would want to play around *with*. In fact, she was the last woman in the world he would want to get involved with. Darrell Sinclair's widow...

Damn it, but Ben needed someone like her.

Mardi caught his scowl, and the brooding faraway look that followed, and bit back the suggestion on her lips. He might be *asking* for her ideas, but he plainly didn't want to hear them. Perhaps it made him feel disloyal to his wife's memory.

Better, she decided, to keep any further ideas for another time...if there *was* another time.

"Let me think about it," she hedged, and he nodded, as if satisfied. "Um, I haven't thanked you for the pie and the cake," she added. "There was really no need...."

"I felt responsible, calling on you at such a bad time.

Hey, kids, leave some for us!" he called out as they reached the terrace. "We want some drinks and nibbles, too."

Ben stuck out his chin. "We've had enough anyway. Come on, Nicky..." He grabbed his friend's hand and dragged him away. "Let's look for snails." They ran down the steps together.

Cain rolled his eyes. "I doubt if they'll find any. Our gardener's very meticulous about snails and weeds."

Yes, she could see that. "How often does he come?" she asked curiously. Any gardening needed at home she'd always done herself. Not that her own garden needed much attention, being mostly native gum trees with a few hardy shrubs.

Darrell, obsessed with his rise up the ladder of success, had never had the time or the inclination for gardening. He'd insisted that their house had to be furnished and decorated before they made any major changes to the existing native garden, and he'd left her with the unpaid bills for those fine new furnishings—with accumulated interest to rub salt into her wounds.

"Our gardener, Joe, comes each day, Monday to Friday," Cain replied. "He has the weekends off."

Five days a week? Mardi blinked. Still, it was the kind of garden, she supposed, that would need constant attention.

"Some orange juice, Mardi?" Cain was pouring a glass for her as he spoke. "Please, sit down. We can watch the boys from here."

We? Mardi flicked an edgy tongue over her lips. He was going to stay out here with her? Or did he intend to make an excuse to escape the minute he'd finished his morning tea?

Cain, eyes narrowed against the sun, noted the nervous gesture. She was obviously uncomfortable with him. Because he was Sylvia Templar's husband and a disquieting reminder of her husband's affair with his wife? Well, he guessed it was understandable that she'd feel a bit uptight. Especially if she'd loved her no-good husband.

He looked into the veiled amber eyes and found himself angry on her behalf, and curious to know more about her.

Leaning back in his chair, he tried to put her at ease. "Well, Mardi, what do you do during the week, when you're not looking after your son and your grandfather? Do you work? Have a career? Play bridge?"

Despite his efforts to be pleasant, a hint of cynicism curved his lips. Most of the rich, Yuppie wives he knew belonged to bridge clubs and lunched together several times a week, when they weren't at the beauty parlor or recovering from yet another glittering social evening or fashion parade in aid of some charity—usually with more emphasis on "social" than "charity."

He saw Mardi's dark eyelashes flutter down, as if the last thing she wanted to do was talk about herself. Surprising, he thought, for a woman.

"I have a part-time job during the school holidays," she said with obvious reluctance, "and during the school term I work at a girls' school. I only worked part-time last year, but I'm hoping to increase my hours this year."

Mardi gritted her teeth, a determined flare in her eyes. Hopefully the school would let her work there full-time. Otherwise she'd have to look for another job, one that paid as well or even better—which wouldn't be easy, since she had no formal qualifications.

"Oh? You're a teacher?"

"No…" She shook her head. "I work in the school office."

"Ah. And during the school holidays?"

It was the question she'd been dreading. Did he really want to know, or was he simply making conversation?

She lifted her chin. Dammit, it was nothing to be ashamed of. If he wanted to be snobbish and disapproving about it, too bad. He wouldn't understand what real need, real desperation, was.

"I've been doing some housecleaning during the week. Grandpa's been keeping an eye on Nicky while I'm out." It was only for a few hours, Wednesday to Friday, but it paid for a few basics. It wasn't helping with Darrell's crushing debts though!

She saw Cain's eyes narrow, a faint gleam intensifying the sharp blue. Now he disdains me, she thought, feeling equal disdain for him. He was just like Darrell. Her image-conscious husband would have had a fit if he'd known his wife had lowered herself—been *forced* to lower herself—to clean other people's houses.

"You have no other relatives? Parents? Siblings?" Cain wondered grimly what kind of financial state her husband must have left her in, for her to have to scrounge around doing menial jobs.

She shook her head. "I lost my parents when I was six. My grandparents brought me up. Grandma died when I was thirteen, after a long illness—" she swallowed "—and I lived with Grandpa until I married Darrell." Not wanting to talk about her husband, she added quickly, "Grandpa came to live with us when he broke his hip and could no longer care for himself."

It was the one compassionate act Darrell had committed, though even that was suspect. He'd sold Grandpa's house for him and put the money into so-called safe stocks, which had crashed, leaving Ernie penniless and dependent on Darrell and herself—and a meager old-age pension. But around the same time Darrell had bought two original oil paintings by famous Australian artists and a couple of expensive Italian suits, and the sneaking suspicion had taken root that he'd stolen Ernie's money for himself.

She'd even accused him outright once, during a bitter emotional clash over his wild spending and the amount of time he spent with Sylvia Templar, but his fury and his vicious threats of legal vengeance if she ever repeated such libel outside their home had frightened her into silence.

"Ernie told me he needs a hip operation," Cain revealed with a faint frown. "He said he's been on a waiting list for months and doesn't know when it will be done. That's pretty tough on an old man in pain."

Tears sprang to Mardi's eyes. She knew how tough it was on Grandpa, but what could she do, without private health insurance? Nicky needed a tonsil operation almost as urgently, and she still had to deal with the massive debts Darrell had left behind.

She blinked and turned away, looking for the boys. At first she couldn't see them and rose anxiously from her chair, afraid they might have scaled the gate at the bottom of the garden and run down to the water. Nicky had been taking swimming lessons before his father's death, but he couldn't swim properly yet. He could barely keep himself afloat without water wings.

And then she saw them, lying on their tummies on the lower lawn, chins resting on their hands, feet waving in the air. She flopped down again with a relieved sigh. "Sorry," she mumbled. "I couldn't see them for a second."

Cain gave her a surprisingly sympathetic look. "You're very protective of your son.... It's good to see."

There was a brooding look in his eye now, making her wonder if he was thinking of his wife Sylvia, who'd left her son with baby-sitters at every possible opportunity—

except when she'd wanted a cover for her clandestine affair!

"Tell me," Cain murmured, puzzled by this woman who was so different from others he'd known. "How did you and your husband first meet? Did you work in the legal profession, like him, before you were married?"

Mardi shook her head. "We met at university. I was halfway through a library science course and Darrell was in the final year of his law degree. We were both members of the uni tennis club."

He'd been so charming and attentive in those days, and she'd imagined she'd found the man of her dreams. He'd loved her then, too—as much as Darrell was capable of loving anyone but himself.

Cain's eyes searched hers. With a library science course behind her, why wasn't she working as a librarian? "You finished your degree?" he asked, not sure why he was so curious to know.

"Unfortunately, no. We got married and had a baby instead."

She became pregnant on the night of Darrell's graduation, during his first year as a fledgling lawyer. He was shocked when she told him. He'd planned a bright future as a commercial lawyer, making lots of money, and having a baby so soon, he said, could hold him back. She'd been determined to keep her baby, even if it meant losing Darrell, but in the end he'd stuck by her, insisting they get married immediately. *I don't want any skeletons in my closet...any mud people can throw at me in the future. What if I go into politics one day?* She would have preferred to think he'd wanted to marry her because she was irresistible, but she'd always known she was no raving beauty, and she was just grateful that this charming, handsome, ambitious young lawyer wanted her to share his life.

Once Nicky was born, Darrell had insisted she stay at home with their child. *I'm not having people saying I can't support my wife.* She'd taught herself to cook and sew instead, determined to do everything in her power to support her husband as he clawed his way up the ladder of success.

It was only when the debts had begun piling up and her son started kindergarten, giving her some free time, that she was able to persuade Darrell to let her go back to work part-time. But she'd had to settle for office work. She wasn't qualified for anything else.

"So you play tennis." Cain wasn't surprised that she'd caught Darrell's eye on the tennis court. She would tan easily, he imagined, and must look very fetching in short white skirts and brief tops. His gaze flickered to the tennis court down below. "We'll have to have a few hits sometime."

Mardi colored. Was he serious? "I haven't played since the early days of…my marriage. I'd be hopeless now. You must play a lot yourself," she said wistfully, "having a court of your own. You must be an expert tennis player." She could just imagine Cain lunging for a forehand, his long powerful legs tanned by the sun, his broad chest and shoulders straining against his white tennis shirt. She stifled a quiver.

He laughed—a short laugh. "I'm afraid I'm pretty hopeless. I had a few lessons after we moved in here, but unless you play consistently and get plenty of practice, you don't get very far."

She was surprised. "You don't use your court regularly?" What a criminal waste!

"I've been so busy working, I seldom have time to play. And my wife rarely played." She hadn't liked getting hot and sweaty and looking less than perfect, Cain recalled with a touch of irony. "She preferred other pursuits during the week…and on weekends she usually had a social function or charity evening to prepare for. *To pamper herself for.* She loved going out. And she loved entertaining. Far more than I did.''

He couldn't believe he was revealing so much. What was it about Mardi Sinclair that was loosening his tongue and his usual inhibitions? Women didn't normally worm out confidences from him. He wasn't the confiding type. Women were far too prone to gossip.

To shift the focus back to her, he rapped out a bald question without pausing to think. ''Did you know your husband was having an affair with my wife?''

Chapter Four

Mardi stiffened. So here it was. The real reason he'd invited her here today. To grill her about his unfaithful wife!

"I had no idea," she said as steadily as she could manage. "I was aware that they knew each other. Our sons, being close friends, often wanted to play together. And with my husband being a lawyer, it didn't seem strange when he told me your wife had asked him for some legal advice and that they needed to meet more often to discuss it."

Cain's dark eyebrows rose. "Legal advice…about what, precisely? Did Sylvia commit some traffic infringement while I was away? Have a dispute with a neighbor? Or with one of our staff?"

Mardi shrugged, chafing at the humiliating memories she'd been trying to blot out. "I never knew. Darrell said it was confidential." What a fool she'd been to trust her husband so blindly. She'd never make that mistake again… be so naively trusting.

"In hindsight," she admitted, dragging the words out, "I'd say it was just a ploy to see more of each other."

No point in mentioning her totally unfounded suspicion that Sylvia might have been seeking advice on a divorce. Having seen the Templars' luxurious home and taken a peek into their glittering lifestyle, it seemed highly unlikely that such an image-conscious, avaricious woman would have wanted to give it all up for a social-climbing, debt-ridden lawyer.

Only, Sylvia hadn't *known* that Darrell was in debt. He'd put on such a brilliant show. No con man could have been more convincing. Mardi shifted in her chair.

"I'm sorry, Mardi. I didn't mean to upset you."

"You haven't upset me." No man, she vowed, would ever upset her again. "I think I'll go down and play with the boys—organize a game or something. They'll only dream up some mischief if I don't—like trampling your lovely plants or churning up your lawn or knocking over one of your statues—and I'm sure you wouldn't want that."

As she rose, Cain heard himself apologizing to her. "I should have planned the day better. Organized an outing somewhere. Organized some entertainment for the boys— a movie or a visit to a playground or something."

Mardi paused, unable to believe her ears. Cain, with a magnificent property like this, couldn't think of a way to entertain his son's friends at home?

"I haven't had much experience looking after kids," he admitted, as if he'd read her mind. "I have a high-powered job that's kept me so damned busy in recent years that I—"

"Then maybe you need to change your priorities," she retorted. If he'd had more time for his family, maybe his wife wouldn't have turned to another woman's husband, and his neglected son might have been a happier, less disturbed little boy.

"That's just what I—" Cain began, but she was gone.

Damn, he thought, giving the leg of his chair a kick. *Well-done, Templar. That's not the way to elicit sympathy from this woman. Why don't you think before you open your mouth?*

He brushed a hand over his brow and noted the sweat gathering there. It was growing damned hot out here in the sun. Why hadn't he suggested they bring their swim togs and have a dip in the pool? Even if her son couldn't swim, he and Mardi would have been here to keep an eye on him.

He had an unwitting image of Mardi in a swimsuit. He'd already seen her long legs exposed, and he was sure the rest of her would be equally enticing. He wondered if he'd be pushing things to suggest it for tomorrow—it was about time he took a whole weekend off and spent it with Ben. But she'd probably want to go looking for a house tomorrow, having wasted all day today.

His brow lowered at the thought. What if she found a house in the next few days, and its location was too far away for Ben to see Nicky on a regular basis—if at all? Ben was looking happier today than he'd ever seen him. He couldn't let Nicky and Mardi slip out of his son's life.

Cain hauled himself out of his chair. He ought to be catching up on his paperwork and making a few phone calls, but Mardi was right about priorities. Ben needed him at the moment more than the damned financial world did—though his partners and business clients might disagree. Still, there had to come a time when a man put his family—his son—ahead of his work.

He'd already achieved the personal wealth and success he'd driven himself into the ground for.... Surely he could ease off a bit? And his original motivation—his father—well, what an empty triumph his hard-won success had turned out to be with *him!* His father had been scathing about his achievements—as scathing as he'd been about his failures in the past. Success, to his father, Cain had discovered too late, meant accomplishment of a totally different kind.

He scowled as he bounded down the steps after Mardi. If she wanted to organize a game with the boys, well, he'd darned well join in, too. He'd show Ben he could be a friend as well as a father.

He found his gaze following Mardi as she ran to the boys on the lawn below, her slender figure and natural grace a pleasure to watch. He saw her pluck something from her tote bag and throw it to Nicky, calling out, "Catch, Nicky!" It was an old tennis ball. Nicky caught it expertly, as if he'd played this game many times before. He threw it to Ben, not quite so expertly, and Ben fumbled and dropped it.

Cain held his breath, seeing himself as a child all over again in Ben, and expecting to hear someone berating his son, or taunting him, for dropping the ball. Nobody did, Nicky calling out, "Sorry, Ben," as Ben retrieved it and threw it back to Mardi.

It was then that Mardi glanced round and saw him.

"Ah, Cain…" She smiled at him, pleased that he'd come to join in their game. "Here…catch!" She tossed the ball to him, expecting him to catch it with ease, as he seemed to do with everything else. He managed to get a hand to it, but mishandled it and saw it bouncing away.

"Sorry…wasn't ready," he muttered, feeling the old need to justify his lack of coordination. He lunged sideways, scooped up the ball and threw it carefully to Ben, who caught it this time, closing his small hands over the ball and gathering it against his chest.

"Good catch," Cain said, and turned back to Mardi, anxious to go before he mucked up their game completely. "Look, I just came down to tell you I need to make a couple of phone calls. Will you be okay with the boys for a while?''

Mardi tried not to show the disappointment she felt. Disappointment for Ben's sake. She'd seen the way the boy's face had lit up when Cain had thrown him the tennis ball, and how the light had now died.

''Nicky's waiting for the ball, Ben,'' she said brightly, bringing Ben's mind back to the game. Ben tossed it, rather too aggressively, sending it way over Nicky's head. She laughed, making light of it. ''Wow, what a throw. Chase it, Nicky. Quickly, before it rolls down the hill.''

Cain blew out a sigh as he trudged back to the house. Ben was showing signs of being a natural at sports...like his grandfather. Even at five years of age, Ben was good at running, good at ball games and had a keen eye and good coordination—all the things Cain had always lacked, to his father's despair and disgust.

Sherman Templar, the finest test cricket spin bowler New Zealand had ever produced, had felt ashamed of his clumsy son and was bitterly disappointed that Cain was never going to excel in any sport. He'd accused Cain of not even trying, but Cain *had* tried—for a time. Until the constant belittling and ridicule had turned him against sports altogether. He'd had other skills he was more interested in pursuing. Determined to prove to his father that he could succeed in his own field of choice, he'd honed his flair for numbers and mathematics to stunning success, first at university, and later in the financial world.

But his wealth and success as a hotshot merchant banker had failed to impress his father, who'd been scathing about his accomplishments. True success, to Sherman Templar, meant personal achievement in the world of sports, not financial success in the cold, calculating world of business.

Cain scowled. Instead of heading for the telephone in his office, he made for the well-equipped gym under the house.

He ignored the state-of-art machines and treadmills and found a box of tennis balls. He began hurling them at the brick wall, and catching them one by one—or attempting to—as they bounced back at him. Then he started throwing them high into the air, trying to catch them as they fell. Simple to most people...

Mardi found herself watching for Cain to come back, but he didn't appear again until he called them in to lunch. It was just as she'd thought. He wasn't interested in spending time with his son—not now that he had a reliable baby-sitter to help keep Ben amused. She felt like gathering Ben in her arms and giving him some of the love and comfort he so badly needed and must secretly long for.

A simple lunch of cold meats, salads, miniature party pies and fresh bread rolls lay spread out on a glass-topped table in a sun-filled room off the huge kitchen. Cain referred to the room as the Nook, though it was far bigger than Mardi's idea of a "nook." Behind the table a floral couch and matching armchair faced a built-in TV set and video player.

Was this where Ben spent lonely evenings watching TV? Safely away from the more formal rooms with their all-white decor and fragile objets-d'art?

Elena flitted back and forth from the kitchen during the meal, bringing in extra food, refilling glasses, removing plates and cleaning up spilled juice and crumbs on the glass tabletop.

The two boys did most of the talking over lunch, giggling and chattering away as they gobbled down their food. The moment they'd finished, Ben tugged at Nicky's hand.

"Come on, Nicky, let's go up to my room and play."

He paused, looking up at Mardi. "You can come up and play, too," he invited, and dashed off with Nicky in tow.

"Well," Cain drawled, "you're honored, Mardi. He's never said that to any grown-up before."

Mardi felt a surge of pity for Ben. Poor kid. No mother, no grandparents, a string of baby-sitters he didn't like and a father who obviously never played with him.

"You don't have to go with the boys—they'll be okay." Cain unfolded his long frame and rose from his chair. "We could sit out in the sun, if it isn't too hot for you."

He had time for *her,* but not for his son? "I came here to spend time with the boys, not to take up *your* time," she said pointedly, though she felt a niggling temptation to go with him, if only to find out what made him tick.

But, of course, he was only being polite. He didn't want to stay with her any more than she wanted to be alone with him...except out of curiosity.

"You're not taking up my time. You don't need to watch over the boys every second, Mardi. They'll be fine in Ben's room for a while. They'll get stuck into computer games. It'll keep 'em quiet for ages."

"Ben has his own computer?" A *five*-year-old?

"He's been on his own a lot. It's helped to keep him amused."

To keep him quiet, more likely. Mardi shot him a cynical look. Nicky, of course, would be spellbound. He'd never played computer games—not at home, at least. Darrell's extravagance had seldom extended to his son.

"Ben asked me to join them, so I will," she said, hoping Cain would get the message. *When your son invites you to play, you don't walk away.* "Where is Ben's bedroom?"

"Up the stairs and first right. There's a bathroom next door."

"Thanks." She darted off.

Cain stifled a sigh as he watched her go, trying not to let his gaze linger on the unconscious sway of her hips. She was miffed at him for not joining in their ball game earlier. And she had reason to be. He was miffed at himself. How would he ever get closer to his son if he couldn't even join in a simple ball game with him? Maybe he ought to join them upstairs.... But Ben had asked for Mardi, not him. He might resent his father butting in and making them all feel uncomfortable.

Hell! What to do? Maybe, if he joined in *properly* this time and showed he could enjoy his son's company as much as Mardi did, Ben would be pleased.

He scowled as the phone rang. With a sigh he reached out a hand. It was one of his partners at the bank, wanting to discuss a deal they were working on together. Normally a weekend call didn't bother him, but today he wished he hadn't answered it. Only, he had, and now it was too late. The intricacies of a complex deal grabbed his attention, and his problems with his son were pushed aside.

When Mardi walked into Ben's room, her mouth sagged open. She'd never seen such a huge bedroom—or playroom—in her life, or so many toys, books and playthings. There were several large toy boxes in a corner, a built-in desk with a computer and keyboard on it, and shelves crammed with computer disks, model cars and neatly stacked children's books. She wondered, with a rush of compassion for Ben, who read him those stories, or if the books were mainly for show.

Surprisingly, the boys weren't sitting at the computer. They were lying on the floor building a road out of narrow wooden blocks. "Will you build us a garage for the cars, Mardi?" Ben said, waving to an impressive array of miniature cars lying scattered about the floor.

Smiling, Mardi dropped to her knees on the carpet, relieved to find it was a practical mottled beige screw-pile carpet, rather than a luxuriously soft, pure white carpet like the one downstairs.

It was well over an hour before she saw Cain again. She was sitting on the floor reading Dr. Seuss's *Green Eggs and Ham* to Ben and Nicky when he strode into the room, carrying a tray of drinks. "Want some cordial?"

"Ye-es!" Ben jumped up and grabbed at a glass, spilling a few drops on the carpet as he snatched it up.

"Careful, Ben."

"It's okay...." Mardi hastily dabbed the spots away with a tissue. "Look...all gone."

Ben shot her a grateful look.

"What about your guests?" his father reminded him, and Ben obediently thrust his glass at Nicky, before reaching for another—making sure he didn't spill it this time. "And Mardi?" Cain prompted. An image of her bent head, with shining strands of golden brown hair falling over her face, was still vivid in his mind, along with the rapt expressions of the two boys as they'd sat listening to her.

"Oh, no thanks." Mardi was already on her feet, slipping the book back into its place on the shelf. She glanced at her watch before turning back to him, glad that she'd already urged the boys to help her pack up the cars and blocks. The room had been a shambles ten minutes ago. "We must go," she said, determined not to outstay their welcome.

"Don't go yet," Ben pleaded. "Can't you stay for dinner?"

She glanced down at him with a smile. "We have to get home and cook Grandpa's dinner. And feed Scoots."

"I wish *I* had a dog," Ben said. "Why don't you bring Scoots with you next time?"

Mardi kept her eyes on Ben, not wanting to see the look of horror on his father's face. She could just imagine Scoots in the immaculately kept garden. He'd demolish it in five minutes flat. "You can come to our place next time," she told Ben. "If it's okay with your father," she added quickly. "But not tomorrow." She spoke gently. "Tomorrow we have to go house hunting."

"I wish you and Nicky could live with *us*." Ben's blue eyes gazed up at her in solemn appeal.

Mardi felt her heartstrings stretch tight. This lovable little boy was the uncontrollable monster no baby-sitter could handle? She felt an overwhelming urge to sweep him into her arms, but she couldn't. She mustn't. She didn't have the right. *Your son just needs some loving*, she felt like crying out to Cain.

"Maybe you could come over the day after—on Monday." She smiled at Ben. Her cleaning jobs weren't until later in the week. At least, she mused thankfully, it was her last week of having to clean other people's houses. The following Monday she'd be going back to her part-time job at the girls' school.

"I wish I could see you and Nicky tomorrow." Ben pouted.

"Mum, *can't* we see Ben tomorrow?" Nicky begged. "Sunday's not a good day to look at houses. You *said*. Everyone's out looking on Sunday."

Mardi glanced from one little boy to the other. They were ganging up on her. And how like her precocious son to quote something she'd said herself. She looked at Cain, expecting him to put his foot down and command his son not to pester her, when she'd already said that tomorrow was out.

But he surprised her by asking mildly, his eyes giving nothing away, "Must you go looking at houses? It's going to be even hotter tomorrow, according to the forecast. You and Nicky could bring your swim togs and have a dip in the pool. It won't matter if your son can't swim. You and I will be there to watch over the boys.''

You and I? Cain intended to join them in the pool? Mardi had to make a fierce effort to damp down the heat that ran up her cheeks at the thought of exposing her body to Cain Templar's hot gaze—or, an even more scorching thought, seeing *his* powerful body exposed.

She declined rather huskily. ''I really must look for a place to live.'' Hadn't Cain had enough of them for one weekend? ''Time's running out. I should have been looking today. It's not easy,'' she gabbled on, ''to find a place with enough room for a child, a grandparent and a large dog.'' *At the right price.* That was the killer. So far, anything half suitable had been far beyond her means.

Cain said nothing. He was frowning now, appearing deep in thought.

''Come on, Nicky,'' Mardi said firmly, taking his glass from him and replacing it on the tray.

Ben flung down his own glass. ''I'll race you down-stairs,'' he challenged Nicky.

''You be careful!'' Mardi said, knowing Nicky wasn't used to stairs.

''No running on the stairs,'' Cain warned, his voice booming after the boys as they rushed out the door.

''No, Dad,'' Ben called back, giggling.

Cain shook his head. But he made no move to follow immediately, reaching out to touch Mardi's arm. ''Before you go...''

She paused, her breath snagging in her throat. The intense blue eyes were deadly serious now, making her wonder what on earth was coming.

''I have a proposition to make,'' Cain said, looking as

surprised by his words as Mardi was. "Don't say anything until you've heard me out."

Mardi's eyes wavered. A proposition? She tilted her chin, her eyes cool, waiting...

"You may have noticed the granny flat at the side of my house," Cain said.

She blinked. She *had* noticed it, as she'd come in. By the look of it, a *luxury* granny flat, the size of an average house. "Yes?" she said carefully, though her heart had picked up a beat.

"Normally we use it as a guest house," Cain went on, "though at one time we had a live-in housekeeper and gardener—a married couple—who used it until they retired and moved up north." He paused. "It's empty at the moment. A complete waste of space. You could move in with your family if you like, and—"

She didn't let him get any further. "It's out of the question." She'd never be able to afford the rent, for one thing. And it was too close to Cain Templar for another—much as she'd love to see more of Ben.

"Besides, you said the boys will get sick of each other after a while," she reminded him. "What will happen then?"

"Now that I've seen them together," Cain said calmly, "I can't see that being a worry. Their friendship, their regard for each other, is genuine. I'm convinced it will last. If they do have the odd spat, I'm sure they'll quickly get over it."

Mardi shook her head. "Cain, no," she repeated. He'd thank her afterward for turning down his offer. He obviously hadn't thought this through. "I'm planning to move farther out, where it won't be so—so expensive." She forced out the admission. "I'm a single mother now, and I don't have my husband's income to rely on anymore.'' She lifted her chin. When had she ever?

Cain frowned. What about her husband's superannuation and life insurance? His savings and investments? Had the rotten cheat's ''expenses,'' as she'd called them, wiped out the lot? Had he left her nothing? And not a word of complaint or criticism from her. Blind, unconditional love... What else could it be? The kind of love you read about... A decent woman's love for a worthless lowlife.

A bemused breath hissed through his teeth. His eyes focused on Mardi's face, noting the proud tilt of her chin, the brave set of her mouth, the soft, lush mouth.... His gaze dwelled there a moment, before flicking away.

''The flat would be rent free,'' he said evenly, adding swiftly, knowing she'd be unlikely to accept charity, ''in return for you doing some baby-sitting after school and cooking our evening meal for us. Both jobs will come with a generous salary, of course. Above award rates.''

Mardi's mind reeled. A rent-free flat and a generously paid job... She was speechless.

''We're desperate.'' Cain appealed to her, looking about as desperate, she thought, as a filthy rich, successful merchant banker, obviously not used to begging, could look. But he was plainly serious. ''I've just sacked our cook— she was totally unreliable. And Elena doesn't cook. Today's lunch was as much as she's capable of.''

Despite herself, Mardi felt an unexpected giggle rising. A giggle tinged with hysteria. ''And you think I'd be a better cook? The only cooking you've seen me doing was burned to a crisp.''

''Only because I kept you at the door. You're obviously capable of producing perfectly edible home-cooked meals. The very fact that you were baking pies and cakes puts you ahead of a lot of other cooks I've known. I have complete confidence in you."

She moistened her lips. She wasn't worried about her cooking skills. She *was* a good cook...normally. "You can't be serious," she said, a faint quaver in her voice. "I have a five-year-old son, an invalid grandfather and a dog. A *big* dog," she reminded him.

He winced slightly. "There's plenty of room here for a dog to run around. And the granny flat has three bedrooms, an eat-in kitchen area and a roomy living room—that should be sufficient room for all of you, shouldn't it? I'll take you to see it now."

The masterful Cain Templar...so sure she would fall in with his plans. Everything inside her cried out, *No! Keep right away from him....* But darn it, *she* was desperate, too, and the offer *was* tempting—too tempting to reject out of hand. A three-bedroom luxury flat, *rent free.* A big garden for Scoots. Pleasant surroundings for Grandpa. A paid job, cooking a couple of extra meals each night and doing some baby-sitting.

Her mind raced on. When school resumed in a week's time, Nicky could go to the local state primary school. He wouldn't be at St. Mark's with Ben, but he'd be able to see Ben every day. And while the boys were at school during the day, she could go on working at her girls' school. She *had* to pay off that huge mountain of debts!

Her teeth tugged at her lip. "If I do take a look at it," she said, "you won't say anything to the boys, will you? I mean, about *why* I'm looking it over. They'll only get excited, and I'm not—not—" She heaved a sigh. *I'm not saying yes yet!* "Are there any stairs in the flat?" she asked, determined not to be seduced too easily. "My grandfather could never manage stairs...."

"There are no stairs," Cain assured her. "I guess granny

flats are designed for grannies who can't manage stairs...or grandfathers with bad hips.'' A slight smile lifted the corner of his mouth. ''You'd have to store or sell most of your own furniture though—the flat's already furnished.''

''It's *furnished?*'' Mardi could feel the last of her objections melting away. All the new furniture back home was about to be repossessed, having been paid for with credit they couldn't afford. The worry of having to replace it had been giving her headaches. Grandpa's bed was his own, but it was old and worthless, and the rest of the furniture—wardrobes, desks and bookshelves—had been built in and would have to remain with the house.

''Fully furnished,'' Cain said, watching her closely. He hadn't missed the flare in her eyes. She didn't *want* her existing furniture, even though it had looked brand-new to him. He wondered why. Maybe it would remind her too much of her husband? She must still love the jerk, despite what he'd done to her. She hadn't said a single word against him.

But then—Cain's expression turned wry—*he* hadn't said a word against Sylvia, either. And love had nothing to do with it.

Hell, he thought violently, wishing suddenly that he'd kept his big mouth shut. What was he doing, wanting to get involved—*more* involved—with the widow of his wife's lover? They'd be a fine pair, living hand in glove. Two people with emotional baggage, scarred by a mutual tragedy. *Hell!*

''Look, maybe we'd better not rush into anything,'' Mardi said.

''Just come and look,'' he urged softly, and steered her out. As he followed her down the stairs it occurred to him that she'd just offered him a way out and he'd ignored it.

Chapter Five

Mardi drove home in a daze. She'd asked Cain to let her sleep on it, but she already knew what her answer would be. The flat was perfect! Smaller than her current house, of course, but perfect. And it was all ready to move in to.

Cain's offer of free accommodation *and* paid work would solve so many of her problems. Or at least *help* to solve them. And *he* probably thought he was getting a bargain—a reliable baby-sitter *and* a new cook!

She would discuss it with Grandpa tonight, and if he agreed, she would call Cain in the morning and accept. Even if it didn't work out, or only lasted a few weeks or months, it should give her a chance to pay off at least some of the crippling debts her husband had left her with.

She scowled, still mad at Darrell for letting their private health insurance lapse. It was so unfair! Grandpa was in continual pain and Nicky kept having recurrent ear and throat infections, each attack more debilitating than the last. And because she was so deeply in debt, she couldn't do a thing about it!

She glanced round at Nicky in the rear seat. He grinned at her and she smiled back, her heart lightening. He'd been grinning from ear to ear ever since they left Ben's. And he didn't even know yet about the possible move to the Templars' granny flat. And he mustn't know...until Grandpa agreed.

She would have to be honest with her grandfather about Cain being Sylvia Templar's husband. She wondered if Grandpa would blame Cain for Darrell's affair and shift his resentment of *that Jezebel* to him. Hadn't she wondered herself what had caused his wife to stray?

Was it possible for the Templars and the Sinclairs to live amicably in such close proximity with this simmering mistrust between them? *She* would handle it, because she *had* to, but Grandpa was another story. *Oh, Grandpa, you have to agree to this.... It's the only way we'll get back on our feet.*

Mardi needn't have worried. When she told Grandpa that Cain's granny flat was just right for them, and that it would be rent free, in return for a bit of cooking and baby-sitting—*paid* work—any objections he might have had died. She began to suspect that Grandpa knew more about the extent of Darrell's debts than she'd thought. She'd tried so hard not to worry him with her problems, or to reveal just how low, how devious, how irresponsible her husband had been.

But most of all, she'd wanted to protect Nicky from the truth about his father.

"If it's not going to worry you, love, living so close to *that Jezebel's* house and having to see her husband and son every day, it's not going to worry me," Grandpa assured her. "*She* can't hurt us anymore. If Nicky's happy about it, that's all that matters." He'd seen the radiance in the boy's face when they'd come home. "You look as if you've lost a weight off your own shoulders too, love…finding a place at last.''

She kissed him on the cheek. "Yes, it is a relief,'' she admitted. She thought of Cain Templar and how he affected her, even knowing now who he was, and she wondered if she doing the right thing, agreeing to move into his granny flat and *work* for him. If she'd had any pride, she would never have considered it.

But Darrell had stripped her of any pride. He'd stripped her of a lot of things, she mused bitterly, glancing round at the bare walls and the furniture that no longer belonged to her. Most important of all, he'd stripped away her trust of men.

She inhaled deeply, before reaching for the phone and dialing—stabbing in the number Cain had given her.

"Cain Templar.''

Mardi's grip tightened on the receiver as his deep, velvety voice rolled right through her. "Cain, are you sure about this offer of yours? Have you thought it through? I mean—what will people say? The widow of the man who seduced your wife and virtually caused her death, moving into your granny flat and *working* for you?''

Her heart quaked as she realized what she was saying.

"They'll think I'm a reasonable, understanding man who cares about his son,'' Cain answered coolly. "And that you feel the same way about *your* son.''

Mardi sat still. It took a moment for his words to sink in. When they did, she felt a quiver of relief. "They'll think you're mad.'' Her voice was a husky squeak. *And they'll think I'm a calculating opportunist, out for all I can get.*

"Maybe it's about time I had some madness in my life.'' Cain's tone was dryly amused. "Mardi, are you calling to accept my offer, or are you having second thoughts? If it's going to be too painful for you, living here, if it's going to continually remind you of my wife's affair with your husband…" But he swept on without giving her a chance to speak. "My wife's gone, Mardi. Your husband's gone. We have to move on. Think of your son. And my son. At least the boys will be happy. I thought that was what mattered most to you."

Cain was reminding her of the reason he'd come to her in the first place—the *only* reason. For the sake of their sons.

"It *is* what matters most to me," she said passionately. "And if *you* haven't changed your mind, I accept your offer," she added quickly, before either of them could come up with any new objections.

"Good. You can start packing your things." Cain's voice was brisk and businesslike. What he *privately* thought she had no idea. "You can move in as soon as you're ready. How long will you need? I'll arrange for a delivery van to drop in some large cartons in the morning. They can help you pack your things, then deliver them when you're ready."

It was like being swept along by a tidal wave.

"I'll need a couple of days," she said, mentally calculating all she would have to do. And somehow she would have to scrape up enough money to pay for the delivery van. "Is it okay if we move in on Tuesday?" She would arrange for her furniture to be picked up from her house the day they moved out.

"Fine with me. You can park your car in my garage. I only have the one car now."

He must have disposed of Sylvia's sporty red model. "You haven't seen my car," Mardi said with a grimace. "You won't mind if it brings down the value of the neighborhood?" At least it would be hidden away in his garage and not sitting out in the street for everyone to see.

"Is it roadworthy? Safe?"

"Oh, it's *safe* enough." She wouldn't carry Nicky in an unsafe car. "It's just old. With a few rust patches."

"Well, we'll have to see how it goes. If you're going to be driving my son around, I'll want to be sure he's in a reliable car."

"I wouldn't drive my own son around in a car that wasn't," she said, bristling.

"No, of course you wouldn't." But he didn't sound convinced. His idea of reliability and hers were no doubt poles apart. Like most things about them.

"I'll look after Nicky and Ben for the rest of today," Cain surprised her by offering. "It'll keep them out of your hair while you start packing. They can keep cool in the pool."

In the *pool?* The boys would have to be watched like hawks, and she wasn't sure she could trust Cain to watch them that closely.

"I—I'd rather Nicky didn't go swimming without me," she faltered. "He's only had a few lessons and he isn't too comfortable in the water yet."

Well, now he knows *I don't trust him.* Mardi held her breath, hoping she hadn't put his back up.

"No worries," he said mildly. "I'll take them to a movie instead. I'll pick up Nicky in an hour. We'll grab some lunch at the mall, then find a suitable kids' movie."

"*You'd* go to a kids' movie?" The disbelieving question leapt out. "It's pure bedlam. Do you know what you're in for?"

"Well, I guess I'll find out," came the droll response.

"It'll do you good," she said.

"That sounds ominous. I'll do my best to endure," he promised solemnly. "See you at eleven."

"He'll be ready." Mardi was surprised at the wry humor in his voice. Did he actually have a sense of humor? She found herself smiling. He'd need it!

Cain sat for a moment after hanging up, sighing deeply. So, the deed was done. She'd accepted his offer. He didn't know whether to feel relieved or dismayed. He felt a touch of both, he decided ruefully.

His mind conjured up an image of Mardi: soft lips, warm hazel eyes and a smile he wished would appear more often. Maybe once she was out of that creep's house, away from the memories that obviously still caused her pain, she *would* smile more.

He wasn't sure why he was so anxious to see her smiling, happy...

Mardi could tell at a glance, when Cain dropped Nicky home later that afternoon, that her bright-eyed son had enjoyed every minute of the all-action kids' movie he and Ben had chosen to see, though Cain shot her a martyred look when she asked how he'd survived it. Glad that he was at least trying, she made him an offer in return, suggesting he drop Ben over the next day on his way to work.

"Grandpa and I will keep an eye on the boys while we go on with the packing and stuff. They'll be fine."

"Are you sure?"

Cain looked relieved, she thought.

When he arrived the next morning with Ben, he was the suave, impeccably dressed merchant banker again, in yet another well-cut suit, this time in a lightweight gray fabric, the perfect choice for a summer heat wave. The casual Cain of the weekend was nowhere in sight.

A shadow darkened her eyes, his dressed-for-success look reminding her of Darrell, the high-flying city lawyer who'd always made sure he was immaculately attired for his determined rise up the ladder of corporate success. The only difference was that Cain had already achieved his wealth and success. And now, it seemed, he was working just as hard to maintain his exalted position.

"I've told Ben he's not to get in your way," Cain drawled, as if he'd caught her look and put it down to the prospect of having to look after two boisterous five-year-olds for the day. "He's to do everything you tell him to. I'll drop by at lunchtime with some chicken and fries—enough for all of you."

Mardi couldn't hide a flicker of surprise. Darrell had never offered to bring food home at lunchtime during a busy working day.

She abruptly cut off the thought. Was she going to compare every man she met with her cheating, spendthrift husband? *Cain's being thoughtful. Appreciate it.*

"You'd have time to do that?" she asked.

"I'll make time," he promised. And then he spoiled it. "If anything urgent blows up at work, I'll get someone else to deliver it. Don't *you* prepare anything."

"No," she said impassively, "I won't." Would he ever put his son first...even before urgent business?

True to his promise, Cain brought over lunch, but he didn't stay to share it, promising to be back for Ben later that afternoon. He could see that the two boys were having the time of their lives together.

Mardi actually gave him a smile, not only for the generous lunch, but for making a special trip from his city office in the middle of the day.

"Ben can have dinner with us, if you think you might not get home until late," she offered impulsively. "We normally have a fairly early dinner."

"I won't be late. Some friends have invited us over for

dinner tonight. But thanks." He gave a flicker of a smile, and then he was gone.

For a few jolting seconds, the aftershock of his dynamic presence and that quick smile lingered. Mardi had no doubt he turned on his charm with every woman. He was that kind of man.

She could almost feel sorry for Sylvia Templar...but she felt no similar softening toward her straying, spendthrift husband.

Cain was on her doorstep again by five o'clock. She'd expected him much later.

"Have they worn you out?" he asked her.

Mardi gave a wobbly laugh and turned away. Did she *look* worn out? She must have a red, sweaty face and dirt smudges on her cheeks and why, oh why, hadn't she brushed her hair and changed her filthy T-shirt before he arrived? He'd be thinking twice about letting her cook for him in his grand house or share the care of his son when she always looked such a mess.

"The boys have been no trouble at all," she assured him, tossing the words over her shoulder as she headed back down the passage to find Ben. "I've managed to get lots of work done. I'll just call Ben for you."

Cain's eyes followed her as she moved away, entranced by her natural grace and lightness of step, even after a hard day's work. A woman with no airs, he thought appreciatively. A pleasant change.

That evening Mardi had a call from Alan Ross, the prep grade teacher at St. Mark's.

"I must apologize, Mrs. Sinclair, for not calling you before, but I've just come back from holidays. I wanted to offer my condolences on your—um—"

"Thank you," Mardi said. She was used to people feeling awkward about Darrell's death.

"I also wanted to remind you," Mr. Ross continued, "that St. Mark's has a holiday program this week, for children starting school next Monday. It's a chance for them to get to know each other in advance...though many, of course, will already know your son from kindergarten."

"Ah, yes." With the trauma of the past couple of months, she *had* forgotten about the holiday program, and Cain Templar had obviously forgotten, too.

"Thank you for the reminder, Mr. Ross, but I—I'm afraid Nicky won't be coming back to St. Mark's this year." *Please don't ask why.*

"But your husband has already paid Nicky's school fees for the year. He—um—paid last November...in advance."

She was speechless. *Darrell* had paid Nicky's fees? She couldn't believe it. "Are you...sure?" How, exactly, had Darrell paid for the school fees? By credit card? With a check that was going to bounce?

"Perfectly sure." No hesitation. "A whole year paid in advance, as I said...paid in cash."

Cash! Her head swam. Where had Darrell found that kind of money? No wonder he'd had no cash left in any of his bank accounts when he died.

Still, the extraordinary fact remained—Darrell had paid Nicky's school fees for the year...the one generous thing he'd done for his son.

"So, you'll let Nicky remain at St. Mark's?" the teacher asked. "And you'll send him to the holiday program tomorrow? And for the rest of this week?"

Mardi gripped the receiver. "Yes, I will," she said, thinking how happy Nicky would be, to be going to St. Mark's after all.

"Well, that's good to hear." Mr. Ross sounded relieved.

"Nicky's young friend Ben will be coming to holiday program tomorrow, too. I've just spoken to his father."

He *had?* But of course... Ben's teacher would have wanted to give his condolences to Cain, too. The Templars and the Sinclairs shared a common tragedy.

She just bet Cain would have jumped at the chance to have Ben minded for the day. Now he wouldn't have to take the day off or bother about staying around to "oversee her move," as he'd offered to do. The boys would no longer be there to need watching.

Cain *did* still take off the day. Not having the boys to keep an eye on, he pulled up his sleeves when the delivery van arrived and threw himself into the chore of unpacking with gusto, ending up as hot and grubby as his new tenant. Grandpa had stayed back at their house to keep Scoots out of the way, and to be there when the repossessed furniture was carted away.

"How much do I owe you?" Mardi asked the deliveryman as he was about to leave. She'd slipped out to a cash converter that morning to exchange a cherished string of pearls—a high school graduation gift from Grandpa—for some urgent cash. She'd already sold her wedding ring and sapphire engagement ring and her few other valuables.

"No charge, ma'am. I owed Mr. Templar a favor."

"You don't owe *me* a favor." She glanced round, but Cain was nowhere in sight. "How much is it, please?"

"Nothing. It's all settled. Bye, ma'am." He scuttled off.

There was nothing she could do but seek out and confront Cain. She found him in the tiny rear courtyard, shifting Scoots's kennel into position. His powerful legs were braced beneath his rolled-up khaki shorts, his strong arms showing muscles she hadn't known were there. As he bent over, his sweat-dampened bush shirt clung to his back, revealing more muscles. Whatever else she thought of him, there was no doubt about it—he was a strong, sexy devil. He looked as if he could crush a rock—or a woman—with ease. Or would those strong, well-shaped hands turn gentle with a woman?

And why was she wondering about irrelevant things like that, for heaven's sake?

Cain straightened. "Scoots can sleep here at night, but this yard's too poky to keep him locked up in here all day. He can have the run of the garden during the day."

The run of his beautiful, immaculate garden? "You won't *mind?*"

He shrugged. "I took your advice and had Joe remove the statues from the lawn, so there's more room now for dogs and kids to run about."

"How much do I owe you for the delivery costs?" she rapped out, refusing to be diverted.

"Nothing. Mike's a friend."

She eyed him doubtfully.

"I've put a lot of work his way." Cain's tone was coolly dismissive. "He was happy to help out. Ah, Elena, you're a lifesaver."

His housekeeper had a tray of sandwiches in her hand, and some cans of ice-cold soft drinks. Still no smile, no expression on her face, Mardi noted.

"Take a breather, Mardi." Cain grabbed a can of drink and a handful of sandwiches before swinging away. "I have to go and speak to Joe about something."

Did he really need to speak to his gardener or was it just an excuse to get away from her? Mardi wondered.

She heaved a sigh, hoping she was wrong, hoping he *had* told her the truth about the work being done for nothing. The last thing she wanted was to be beholden to Cain Templar. *In any* way.

Mardi was unpacking glasses when he came back.

By late afternoon, when the bulk of the unpacking and sorting was finished and both she and Cain were dripping from the summer heat and exhaustion, he suggested a dip in the pool before they picked up the boys from school. Mardi intended to go home afterward to do a final cleanup at her by-now-empty house and to fetch Grandpa and Scoots.

But the thought of throwing herself into cool, refreshing water was too heavenly to resist. "Well, just a quick dip...."

"Grab your togs and join me there."

Mardi darted into her bedroom and snatched up a one-piece bathing suit from a pile of clothes on the double bed, then slipped into the bathroom to find a towel. After retying her ponytail, which had come loose, she hurried out to the pool.

Cain was already there. She could see him slicing through the water, his dark head and powerful tanned arms all she could see. He sure could swim!

While he was heading for the far end, away from her, she slipped into the water at the shallow end, gasping a little as her hot body hit the cool blue water.

It felt wonderful.

She did a few experimental forays at her end of the pool, not being the expert swimmer Cain was. He was on his way back now, the length of the pool obviously no real challenge to him. When he pulled up beside her, shaking water from his hair and eyes, he was barely puffing.

"Just don't suggest a race," she begged. "I've never been much of a swimmer. I suppose you were university champion?"

"I never swam competitively." Did his eyes cloud for a second? "Besides, I'm too pooped to suggest a race."

She didn't believe him. He looked as if he could have done several more laps without any trouble at all. She found her gaze riveted to him, the sight of his glistening tanned shoulders and sleek wet hair mesmerizing her for a second—until he reached out a hand and brushed his fingers across her cheek.

It was so unexpected she jerked back, her damp skin suddenly on fire.

"You had some hair in your eyes," he said, his hand dropping away. He'd felt a sharp reaction himself to the cool softness of her cheek, her skin smooth and damp under his fingers. Angry with himself, he was quick to mask any expression. If this arrangement of theirs was going to work, he didn't want that kind of complication. And neither would she.

"I'll do one more lap, then I'll go and get dressed." He almost ground the words out. "You take your time, Mardi. When I pick up Ben, I'll tell Nicky you're on your way. Oh, and I don't expect you to cook our evening meal on your first night here. I'll rustle up something myself."

He streaked off through the water, and she was left feeling mildly rebuffed. She could have kicked herself. Why had she recoiled like that? He must have noticed. She just hoped he'd put it down to an instinctive reaction, or even distaste at being touched by a man, and not stupidly think she was reacting physically…to him!

She breaststroked a few yards, then turned and swam back toward the shallow end to avoid facing him. A moment later she heard him emerging from the pool in a whoosh of water, but she didn't turn around, pretending not to notice.

After he was gone, she cursed under her breath. She hadn't even thanked him for taking the day off to help her.

Chapter Six

After dropping the two boys off at St. Mark's the next morning, Mardi went off to her Wednesday cleaning job, leaving Grandpa and Scoots to settle into their new surroundings.

When she came home around midday, Grandpa was dozing in his favorite outdoor rocking chair and Scoots had dug holes in the perfect garden.

Appalled, she stared at the unsightly holes, the scattered earth, the damage to Cain's plants.

"Scoots, you're a bad boy!" The Lab, knowing he was in trouble, slunk behind an exotic shrub—one that was still in one piece. "Come on, you're going back to your kennel!"

She marched him off to the tiny courtyard behind the flat and closed the gate on him. There wasn't much damage he could do there—the entire area was paved, with a few large potted plants in safe corners. "You stay there. If you're good I'll take you for a walk this afternoon, after I've picked up the boys from school."

Scoots pricked up his ears at the word "walk" and wriggled in anticipation.

Mardi hurried back to the scene of the crime. As she was frantically scooping back the disturbed earth with her hands and trying to resurrect the sorry-looking plants, a man in a battered cap and old gardening clothes appeared from the far side of the house. Uh-oh, she thought, Cain's gardener.

"Did your dog do that?" he boomed when he saw the damage. "Ernie told me he was keeping an eye on 'im."

Ernie, she noted. If he and Grandpa were on first-name terms already, maybe Joe would make allowances....

She smiled up at him. "I'm sorry, Joe—it *is* Joe, isn't it?—my grandfather's an old man with a bad hip, and he falls asleep easily. I'm Ernie's granddaughter...Mardi Sinclair."

Joe grunted. "You'll have to control your dog better," he growled. "Just as well Mrs. Templar's not here no more. She'd be having a fit." He noticeably shuddered.

Mardi sighed at the reminder of Sylvia Templar. Her presence was everywhere here, inside the house and out.

"I'm sure Scoots will settle down," she said, "once he becomes more familiar with the place. He's probably a bit confused at the moment, and was trying to stake out his territory."

Joe looked unimpressed.

"The boys will keep an eye on Scoots when they come home from school," she assured the gardener, who merely grunted again and set about repairing the damage himself, virtually nudging her aside. She retreated to the granny flat to prepare lunch.

While inside, the phone rang.

"Ah, Mardi. Cain."

"Oh, hullo, Cain." She felt a prickle of guilt. "Oh, Cain, I'm really sorry, but Scoots dug holes in your garden today while Grandpa was asleep, but don't worry, I've repaired the damage with Joe's help. I've scolded Scoots and locked him up, and I'm going to take him for a walk this afternoon to get rid of some of his—"

"*Whoa!* Hold on! Look, I'm sure you have the matter in hand, Mardi. I'm just calling to let you know that Elena's done some food shopping for me, and you'll find all the ingredients for a roast dinner—leg of lamb, potatoes, vegetables, fruit and other stuff. Why don't you cook the roast for all of us, and we can eat it at my place? Silly for you to cook two separate meals when we'll have more than Ben and I can eat."

Her head spun. She'd been so hyped up about defending Scoots that it took a moment for his words to sink in. Cain wanted them to *eat* together? All *five* of them?

"You're planning to be home early?" she said, surprised. *"Again?"*

"I am. I know you like to eat early. And besides," Cain added, "I'm expecting a delivery. We can eat on the kitchen patio. It's shady out there and quite pleasant in the evenings. And the boys will be able to relax better there than in the house."

You mean you'll be able to relax better, knowing they're not messing up your spotless house, she thought. "Well, if you're sure…" She recalled the touch of his cool fingers on her cheek and her reaction to his touch and felt a quiver of panic. "You're not afraid you'll be creating a precedent," she ventured, "and the boys will expect us to eat together every night? Because—"

"Eating together every night won't be possible," came the curt rejoinder. "I'm often home late or tied up at a business dinner. But since you'll be minding Ben when I'm not at home," he reminded her, "I might have to ask you to give my son his dinner, and maybe even a bed, on those occasions.''

A timely reminder that she was just his cook and Ben's baby-sitter.

''And what about *your* dinner—when you come home late, I mean?'' she asked sweetly. Did he expect her to run around after him at all hours?

''I'll either grab something on the way home—unless I'm going out to dinner—or I'll heat the leftovers in the microwave when I get home.''

''You often don't have dinner with your son?'' she asked tentatively, unable to keep a touch of censure from her voice. Another similarity, she mused darkly, between Cain Templar and her husband. She and Nicky and Grandpa had often eaten alone, too.

But poor Ben must have been forced to share many of *his* evening meals alone with his latest baby-sitter.

''I'm afraid it's the pressure of the job I'm in'' came the brusque reply. ''Long hours, complex negotiations—often interstate or overseas—and deadlines to meet. But you're right,'' he conceded with the hint of a sigh, ''I'll have to make more time for my son. He only has me now.''

Mardi pursed her lips. Had he realized, finally, how much his son needed him?

''I'll be home around five—six at the latest,'' Cain promised, and hung up. He sat for a moment, frowning at the timbered walls of his office. He'd heard the note of reproof in Mardi's voice as she'd queried him about how often he'd had an evening meal with his son. Why did this woman always give him the uncomfortable feeling that she cared more about his son than he did? Damn it, Ben meant everything to him. It was why he'd been working his butt off for years. To make sure his son had every possible advantage in life.

* * *

Just after five, while Mardi was in Cain Templar's kitchen putting scrubbed potatoes and chunks of pumpkin into the oven to bake, Cain breezed in. She gave him a welcoming smile—another early homecoming! He *was* making an effort.

"Where are the boys?" he asked, his nose twitching at the delicious aroma of roast lamb and onions. An apple pie, which she'd baked earlier, sat cooling on the top of the stove. No sign of a charred crust! He licked his lips.

"They're in the garden playing with Scoots. They have strict instructions to keep him off the garden beds," she was quick to assure him. "And Grandpa's keeping an eye on all of them." *Unless he'd nodded off again.*

"Good." Cain was already heading for the door—relieved, no doubt, that she had her dog under control. "I'll just go and change. That delivery I mentioned should be here any minute."

She wondered what it was. A new crystal chandelier? A new state-of-the-art sound system? *Some new fencing to keep Scoots off his neat garden beds?*

She heard a large van pull up outside just as Cain reappeared in faded blue jeans and sneakers, with his white business shirt open at the neck and the sleeves rolled up. He looked so relaxed and athletic and... Mardi gulped, trying not to think about how sexy he looked, but her body was treacherously aware of it.

"Good, they're on time," he said, and ducked out again, leaving her staring after him for a tremulous moment.

A minute later two men in overalls appeared round the side of the house, carrying—of all things—a child's slide! Mardi stood watching wide-eyed through the kitchen window as a double swing followed, then a huge jungle gym, in various pieces. She could hardly believe that Cain had actually acted on her suggestion—and so quickly. But that was Cain Templar. A man of decisive action.

Cain was directing the men to an area near the shaded patio, where they planned to have dinner. Being only visible from the kitchen side of the house, the dark green and bright red swings and monkey bars wouldn't spoil the aesthetics of the manicured front garden! She was relieved to see a pile of tan bark on standby, ready to spread over the area to provide a soft landing if a child fell.

The two boys came running, with Scoots at their heels, to see what the commotion was all about. They gave hoots of delight when they saw what had arrived.

"Wow! A playground! Oh, boy!"

Mardi saw Ben glance up at his father with a look of awed disbelief, and she swallowed hard, pressing her hands to her chest to suppress a strange ache. The boy really loved his father, but he wasn't yet sure of his father's love for him. A thoughtful gesture like this had to be a good start. She smiled at Cain.

The arrival of the play equipment set the tone for the evening. The boys could talk of nothing else, and eagerly gobbled down their meal with Cain's promise that if they ate all their vegetables, and their apple pie and ice cream to follow, they could go and try out their new playthings, which would by then be securely in place. Even Grandpa was in good humor, and didn't mention *that Jezebel* once.

Mardi had set the long outdoor table, and Cain was the perfect host, even producing a bottle of wine for the adults. He kept the conversation rolling with questions about the boys' holiday program, a concerned inquiry about Ernie's bad hip and comments on the news of the day. As they lingered over their wine and dessert, the boys rushed off to play.

Mardi began to think that her decision to come and live here hadn't been such a mistake after all.

As the sun sank low in the cloudless summer sky, Cain rose at last. Ernie had already left, refusing help on the short walk back to the flat.

"That was a great meal, Mardi," Cain said, gathering up a handful of glasses and following her into the kitchen. "Mind if I leave you to clean up? I have some work to do." He looked apologetic, but *was* he? Or couldn't he wait to escape?

"No, that's fine. I'll keep an eye on the boys from the kitchen," she told him.

They'd been warned to be careful and not to swing too high or to do anything silly—especially Nicky, with his breakable glasses—but being only five and liable to show off, both boys still needed careful watching.

Cain paused before striding off. "I have to fly down to Melbourne tomorrow for a couple of nights. Do you think Ben could stay with you, Mardi, while I'm away? I know he'd be happier with Nicky than with a strange baby-sitter."

She glanced up at him, but his face was bland. Had this been his motive all along? "I'll be glad to look after Ben," she said warmly. "There are two beds in Nicky's room.... He'll be happy to sleep there?"

"He'll jump at it. I'll pack a bag for him and drop it in before I leave in the morning. You have a key to my house if you need anything from there."

A high-pitched ringing sound intruded. Cain pulled a mobile phone from his pocket and clamped it to his ear. "Cain Templar. Ah, Tiffany. All set for tomorrow? Good. What's that? Oh, no need for that. We can talk about it on the plane. I'll pick you up at 8:00 a.m. Yes. Fine. See you."

He raised a hand to Mardi as he left the kitchen. "Thanks again for dinner, Mardi. See you in the morning."

"You're welcome." Her eyes followed him, a faint frown wrinkling her brow. Tiffany? He was taking a *woman* with him to Melbourne? Was Cain in the habit of inviting females along on his business trips? To help him wile away his free evenings perhaps? *Or was his trip to Melbourne nothing to do with business at all, but just an excuse to spend a couple of nights alone with his latest floozy, away from the watchful eyes of his young son?*

And why the heck should it bother *her,* one way or the other?

Cain dropped his bag in the hall at the end of the week and went straight to the granny flat to announce his arrival home. Mardi and the two boys were in the kitchen having a late Saturday-morning breakfast.

"Home already?" she commented, carrying her empty cup to the sink. "How was the trip?"

His eyes followed her, drinking in her supple grace as she moved. She'd pulled her hair back in a rubber band and wore no makeup, not even lipstick. Not that she needed it. Her lips were pink and lush enough without it.

"It achieved its purpose," he answered. As she turned back, his gaze grew speculative. She looked tired, he thought. The lovely hazel eyes had dark smudges underneath and there were lines of strain round her mouth. He hoped Ben hadn't put them there. "The boys haven't been too much for you, I hope?"

"No. They've been good as gold," she assured him.

Relieved, Cain turned to smile at his son, but Ben's dark head was bowed over his bowl of cereal. He didn't glance up.

But Nicky did. "We had to take Grandpa to hospital in

the night," he announced. "We were there for hours and hours."

"What happened?" he asked. "Is Ernie all right?" No wonder Mardi looked tired.

She seemed to hesitate, busying herself at the kitchen sink. "He had a fall during the night. I was afraid he might have broken something, so I took him to the hospital. I couldn't leave the boys here so I took them with me. The emergency room was very busy and we had to wait for hours. That's why the boys slept in this morning."

Cain glanced at Ben. He was eating his cereal as if his life depended on it, his nose almost buried in his bowl.

Mardi's voice drew his gaze back to her. "Luckily, Grandpa hadn't broken anything, but he was in a lot of pain." She could almost feel her grandfather's pain. She'd hoped the hospital might admit him on the spot and go ahead with his hip operation, but they hadn't. They hadn't even kept him overnight. They'd told him to go home and rest for a few days and they'd let him know when a bed became available. As they'd been saying for weeks. *Months.*

"How's his pain now? Any better?" It was criminal, Cain thought, the way public patients were kept waiting for a bed.

"He says it is, but when he moves—" She winced, compassion for her grandfather welling inside her.

"They're inhuman." Cain glowered. "They should have kept him in emergency until a bed became available." His frown deepened. The vibes coming from Ben were so strong now he had to ask. "How did it happen? Did Ernie trip over something in the night?"

Ben made a choking sound. "I w-won't do it again, Daddy, I promise!"

"Won't do *what* again?" Cain's blue eyes pierced his son's anguished face.

"Leave anything lying around again," Ben wailed. "I promise! I d-didn't mean to do it!"

"Of course you didn't." Mardi moved swiftly to his side, slipping an arm around the boy's quivering shoulders. "It was just a tiny Matchbox car." She defended him. "Easy enough to miss when tidying up. Ben didn't realize how careful we have to be around Grandpa. He feels really bad about it." *So don't make it any worse for him,* her eyes warned Cain.

Cain reined in his rising anger. She was right. Ben knew he'd done the wrong thing and felt wretched enough as it was. "Well, as long as he's learned his lesson."

Ben pushed his plate away. "I've finished." He cast an appealing look up at Mardi. "Can I go and play on the monkey bars now?"

"I've finished, too." Nicky scraped back his chair. "Can I go, too?"

It was Cain who answered. "Yes, off you go."

"And remember to hold on tight," Mardi called after them. She expected Cain to take his leave, too, but he stayed put, filling the kitchen with his virile presence. He'd worn casual clothes for his flight home—a pair of light-colored pants and a darker sports shirt.

"Have you had breakfast?" she asked as she cleared away the dishes. She felt ridiculously nervous. Being alone with Cain, she guessed. Feeling exposed without any makeup and more of a plain Jane than usual. Whatever she thought of him, however like her cheating, immoral husband Cain Templar might be, she wasn't immune to him, she realized bleakly—or her body wasn't. Every nerve end was pricklingly aware of him.

"I had it on the plane, thanks." She saw his chest heave.

"Mardi, you can't let Ernie go on like this. His fall was my son's fault...*my* fault for foisting him on you. I feel responsible. Let me help you with Ernie's operation. At a private hospital."

"No!" The refusal was sharp and immediate. "Thanks."

"I'm not offering you charity, Mardi, simply a loan. A loan you can pay back when you can. No time limit—I know things have been difficult for you."

Mardi averted her face, torn between accepting his offer, so that Grandpa could be relieved of this endless waiting in pain, and throwing the offer back in Cain's face. A *loan*...another debt...it was out of the question. A major operation in a private hospital would cost *thousands*. She'd never be able to pay Cain back!

"Mardi? Please, don't let pride stop you—"

She swung round, her eyes blazing. "I said no!" She gulped in a steadying breath. "I can't accept money from you...as a loan or any other way. We'll wait for a bed. It can't be long now. They've seen how much pain he's in. At least it's eased a bit now."

"Well, is there anything else I can do? If you'd like me to stay with him today while you go out... If you need to do any shopping or just want a break..."

She shook her head. "I did some food shopping yesterday, after I picked up the boys. There's really nothing you can do, thanks—unless you'd like to keep an eye on Ben and Nicky for a while." Now that, she thought, would do Cain good—and his son, Ben, too. "I'll stay here and watch over Grandpa."

"You need a break," Cain persisted. "Isn't there someone—a friend, or a relative—who can come and sit with your grandfather for a few hours?"

"Well, as a matter of fact, Grandpa's having an old friend coming for Sunday lunch tomorrow. He insists that he still wants Albert to come. They're very old friends, and they love reminiscing about old times."

She glanced toward the window, but the boys had already disappeared. "It'll give me a chance to do something with the boys tomorrow. With Nicky, I mean," she amended, remembering that she wasn't responsible for Ben while Cain was home.

Cain moved a step closer. "If Ernie has a friend coming for the day, you won't need to stay at home tomorrow, will you? As long as you leave the old guys some lunch, presumably?"

The clear hazel eyes swung back. "What do you mean?"

"How would you like a relaxing day on the harbor? The boys, too, of course. I've chartered a boat for the day."

Her heart leapt. It sounded like heaven.

"It's a sort of celebration," Cain explained. "The partners at my bank and their families are getting together to celebrate a successful merger we've just finalized in Melbourne."

In Melbourne? So it *had* been a genuine business trip. Mardi glued an impressed smile on her face, while inside she felt something sink. He wasn't inviting just her and the two boys for a relaxing spin on the harbor.... His high-flying partners and their families would be there, too. It must be a *big* boat he'd chartered for the day. Her dreamy vision of an intimate little runaround for just the four of them evaporated.

"You don't have to invite Nicky and me," she hedged. "We won't know anyone."

"You will by the end of the day. Besides, Ben won't want to go without Nicky, and I'll need you to help me with them. As host, it'll be hard to watch the boys and mingle at the same time. We'll be having lunch on board," he coaxed. "We'll anchor off a safe beach and all the kids can go for a swim. It should be very pleasant, especially at this time of year.''

So he wanted her to help him with the *boys*. It wasn't simply an invitation out of the goodness of his heart. What else, she wondered, would he want her to do?

"You'd like me to prepare the lunch, too?" she asked.

"No! Certainly not. I've hired a chef for the day. And drink waiters. You'll be one of the guests—*my* guest."

What would his illustrious work colleagues think of *that?* Or would he make it clear to them that she was the hired help?

"Mardi, please don't say no." His voice brushed over her like soft velvet. "You'll enjoy it." He paused. "You must miss all that."

"All what?" Her eyes flicked upward.

"Well, the social interaction, a chance to gossip, mixing with the kind of people you must have been mixing with before."

With Darrell's Yuppie legal crowd, he meant. With the social set. Cain saw her as a frivolous society wife…like his wife, Sylvia. A fun-seeking social butterfly who'd fallen on hard times since losing her husband.

"I've been too busy to think about what I might be missing," she said with a shrug.

"Quite. You need a day out."

"Okay, you can stop twisting my arm. If Grandpa's okay about me leaving him for a few hours, I'll come. *We'll* come," she said, not looking at him.

Chapter Seven

The boat picked them up the next morning at Cain's private landing stage below the house.

"Wow!" Nicky gaped. "Is that *our* boat?"

"That's it," Cain said, waving the boys aboard.

Mardi tried to look nonchalant, as if luxury motor yachts were nothing new to her. But she had to swallow before murmuring, "Yes, very nice." She was glad she'd decided to wear her cool aqua sundress rather than the shorts and T-shirt she'd hesitated over.

The partners' wives would no doubt be dressed to the nines in the latest designer sunwear, doing their best to outdo one another.

Cain, though, *had* chosen to wear shorts—white shorts that showed off the deep tan of his legs, with a loose-fitting top. Even casual as he'd chosen to be, he looked magnificent, like a dark-haired Greek god, his eyes intensely blue in the glowing morning sunlight.

"Coming on board?" he invited, offering her a helping hand. "We're picking up the others at Dawe's Point." His gaze lingered on her hair as she brushed past him. This was the first time he'd seen her wearing it loose. It made her look softer, more feminine, the sun picking up golden highlights. He liked the sundress she was wearing, too. Very feminine.

As soon as they boarded, the boat moved off, the engines a muffled purr. There were several decks—the main deck, with its sumptuous salon and dining area and covered sundeck at the rear, the captain's bridge on an upper deck, a small sundeck above that, and roomy cabins and a modern galley down below.

Sheer luxury! It must have cost Cain a fortune, Mardi reflected.

The thought of all that money being swallowed in a day's entertaining on the harbor, when she needed money so desperately to care for Grandpa and Nicky and to pay off Darrell's debts, dampened her spirits somewhat. It seemed so unfair that some people had money to burn while others were struggling to survive.

But she mustn't think like that! How could she enjoy the day if she did? And she was determined to enjoy it, and to make it as enjoyable for the boys as she could. Tomorrow they'd be starting their first year at school and she'd be going back to work at the girls' school.

"You look pensive, Mardi," Cain murmured. "Are you wishing that things were as they used to be, that you were out here on the harbor with your husband instead of strangers, and that Darrell had never met my wife?"

She jerked her head round, a cold shudder trembling through her. She'd lost faith in her husband, and most of her feeling for him, long before he'd met Cain's wife.

"But he *did* meet your wife, didn't he?" she said soberly. She glanced up at him. "How do *you* feel about that,

Cain?'' she asked, turning the tables on him. "Do *you* wish things were as they used to be…before they met?''

"Hell, no. I'd want things to be vastly different.'' There was no emotion in his voice, no expression in his eyes, just a cool remoteness. Was that an admission that he'd played around, and that he bitterly regretted it? Or an admission that their life together hadn't been happy anyway?

"Different in what way?'' she asked.

"In every way.'' There was a chilling finality about his answer. "Come up and meet the captain, Mardi. The boys will be fascinated by all the instruments and gadgets and screens.''

The minutes flew by very pleasantly, and before she knew it they were at Dawe's Point, pulling into the wharf in the shadow of the massive Sydney Harbor Bridge. Her tension crawled back. It would have been far more relaxing to spend the day with Cain and the boys than meeting a bunch of strangers—rich merchant bankers and their society wives.

Mardi watched from the rail as several couples, some with children, began to board, noting that most of them were dressed as casually as she and Cain.

There was no way-out designer gear in evidence, no gaudy jewelry, though an expensive gold watch flashed in the sunlight.

Her tension eased a trifle.

"Where's Tiffany?'' Cain asked when they were all on board.

Mardi stiffened. He'd invited *Tiffany* to join them? The woman he'd taken to Melbourne? And the others *knew* her?

"You know what Tiffany's like—always one to make a grand entrance,'' one of the men commented with a wink. "She'll turn up in a minute—she's not going to miss this celebration.''

Ah, yes, Mardi remembered. Today was a celebration. An important merger had been signed, sealed and delivered. And Cain had been responsible for it.

"Well, let's have a drink while we wait." Cain nodded to a drink waiter, who hurried forward with a tray of glasses filled with champagne. Another waiter had soft drinks and beer. Mardi accepted a glass of mineral water. There'd no doubt be wine with lunch, and she was determined to keep a clear head.

As everyone milled around, a few grabbing deck chairs to sit in, others already spreading into the salon and to other parts of the boat, Cain dragged her over to the nearest group and introduced her, beckoning to Nicky and Ben to join in.

"I'd like you to meet Mardi Sinclair and her son, Nicky, Ben's best friend. You know my son, of course. Mardi looked after Ben while I was in Melbourne this week. The two boys are inseparable and Mardi often helps out with Ben."

Helps out with Ben... At least he hadn't embarrassed her by introducing her as a friend, which she wasn't.

She held her breath, wondering if Cain would add that she was living in his granny flat and doing some cooking for him. But he didn't, reeling off the names of his colleagues and their wives instead.

"Here's Tiffany now," someone called out, and all heads turned toward the wharf, Mardi's included. One of the husbands whistled, and his wife nudged him in the ribs.

Mardi felt her breath catch. A shapely suntanned figure in a skimpy hot pink top and a flowing magenta skirt slashed to the thigh was sashaying toward the boat, waves of gleaming black hair tumbling over her bare shoulders. She wasn't hurrying, plainly relishing the impact she was making on those watching.

Mardi's eyes opened wide, then narrowed, her spirits, for

some reason, plummeting. Tiffany was a stunner; there was no other word for it.

As Tiffany strutted up the gangway steps, something inside Mardi rebelled. She wasn't going to play the helpless, self-pitying widow. She would hold her head high and smile. Why should she care what type of woman Cain was attracted to? If he wanted another femme fatale like his wife, he deserved all he got.

Cain reached Tiffany first as she stepped onto the deck. Mardi turned away as he bent his head to give her a kiss of greeting.

"Like to go up to the top sundeck, boys?" Mardi asked, eager to escape. They nodded and ran on ahead of her.

There was no one else on the small upper deck. Squawks of laughter rose from the deck below, where the older children had gathered. Mardi leaned over the rail, turning her face into the breeze to watch the boats on the harbor and the spectacular Sydney Opera House as they passed by. In time, the high-rise city buildings gave way to sprawling harborside homes jutting from the rugged sandstone banks.

"There's the Manly ferry!" squawked Ben. "That's the ferry we went on last week!" The school had taken the boys for a trip on the harbor.

It was a while before they saw Cain again. When he joined them on the upper sundeck later, Mardi tensed. He had Tiffany with him. Not just *with* him—Tiffany's red-tipped fingers were hooked possessively round his arm. There was no sign of a wedding ring.

"Ah, there you are, Mardi." Cain eased himself free. "You're the only one who hasn't met Tiffany."

Mardi braced herself to look at the woman beside him. Their eyes met, clear hazel clashing for a second with dense dramatic black. Tiffany's expression and body language were indifferent, even bored, as if she had no desire to meet this insipid nobody Cain had dragged along for the day.

Cain's tone was smooth as he introduced his glamorous companion. "I'd like you to meet Tiffany Carr-Jones, Mardi, one of our partners at the bank. She and I worked together on this merger we've just clinched in Melbourne."

Tiffany was a *partner?* And she'd gone to Melbourne with him as a *business* colleague? Mardi tried not to show the shock she felt. So this flamboyant creature was no bimbo, no mere sex object; she was an intelligent, highly skilled merchant banker as well as a stunning beauty. Her spirits plummeted even further.

"Mardi Sinclair." As Cain introduced her, his lips curved in what, for him, was a smile. Slight as it was, it caused her heart to pick up a beat. "My son and Mardi's son, Nicky, are best friends," he explained to Tiffany. "They both go to St. Mark's. Mardi often looks after Ben for me."

A furrow appeared between the perfectly arched brows. "Sinclair?" She pounced on the name. "You can't mean *that* Sinclair?" Her eyes sharpened as they pierced Cain's. "She's not the *widow?*" Though she'd dropped her voice, the question was perfectly audible to Mardi. When Cain didn't deny it, Tiffany gave a disbelieving laugh. "You have that back-stabbing lawyer's widow as Ben's *baby-sitter?*"

Cain shrugged, as if it were neither here nor there. "Our sons play together. Go to school together. Do everything together. They're inseparable. Whatever was between our spouses is irrelevant."

Tiffany pursed her glossy red lips. "With your sons so inseparable, and a baby-sitter on tap, you must see a lot of the boy and his mother. They live nearby?"

Now it was Cain who frowned. He didn't like being interrogated, even by a close colleague. *How* close, Mardi preferred not to think about.

"Mardi and her family have rented my granny flat."

Rented, Mardi noted, bemused. So he wasn't going to reveal their true situation—that he'd taken pity on the poor widow and waived any rent. Was he trying to save her feelings? Or avoid any embarrassment to himself?

"Well, lucky them," Tiffany purred, but Mardi could feel the claws underneath.

"Living in the flat makes it convenient for Mardi to look after Ben, and also to do some cooking for us. It's a business arrangement," Cain spelled out, in case Tiffany had any ideas it might be anything more.

"Ah." His husky-voiced colleague seemed slightly appeased. "Well, I'm glad you've found a reliable cook and baby-sitter, Cain." Her dark eyes flicked over Mardi as if domestic service was all she was fit for. "It must be a load off your mind to know that your son is being looked after when you're not around."

And a load off yours, too, no doubt, Mardi thought in contempt. Tiffany obviously had little feeling for Cain's son.

She turned away, then gave a choked cry. "*Ben,* get down off that rail!" She flew across the deck. "You mustn't climb the rail," she scolded as she dragged him down.

Cain's shadow fell over her. "Ben," he rasped, "you know what the safety rules are on board a boat."

"Sorry, Dad." Ben hung his head. "I was holding on tight," he defended himself.

"Not good enough. What if Nicky had tried to copy you and fallen overboard? What if the boat had lurched suddenly and thrown you *both* overboard?"

"Oh, don't growl at him, Cain," begged a honeyed voice

from behind. Tiffany, slinking forward, gave Ben a melting smile that failed, Mardi noted, to reach or soften her dark eyes. "Your baby-sitter was meant to be watching him, wasn't she? It's not the poor kid's fault. He's only four."

"I'm five and a half," Ben scoffed. He looked up at his father. "It wasn't Mardi's fault. I'll be good for Mardi, I promise." There was apprehension in his eyes now, as if he were afraid his father might send Mardi packing, like the baby-sitters he'd had before.

"I know you will." Cain patted his son on the shoulder. As his eyes veered to Mardi's, a quiver riffled through her.

"Well, now that you've sorted things out, Cain, can we go down and join the others?" Tiffany's voice held a fractious note. "They'll be wanting to hear more details about our merger."

"Sure. Let's go down," Cain agreed. "It's almost time for lunch anyway. Are you coming down with the boys, Mardi?"

"We'll be down in a minute," she said, not wanting to trail after Cain and Tiffany like a dutiful Mary Poppins with her charges.

By the time Mardi followed with Nicky and Ben, lunch was being served, buffet-style, in the dining salon, with a succulent array of seafood, chicken, salads and other delicacies, and wine flowing freely.

The partners and their wives were pleasant enough to her when they came into direct contact, but Mardi still felt like the odd one out, as if she didn't belong in this elite, close-knit group, where everyone knew one another so well.

The men talked mostly about money and shares and business takeovers—subjects of no interest to her—while the women's conversation focused on clothes, diets, fashion parades, beauty treatments and the next big social event or latest hit show in town, which of course she hadn't seen.

Cain tried to include her as much as he could, but people kept claiming his attention. Mardi found herself backing away with the excuse that she had to "keep an eye on the boys."

As soon as the meal was over, a dinghy began ferrying to the safe beach anyone who wanted a swim. Mardi bundled the boys into the dinghy, then watched from the sand as they played in the shallows with the other children.

As the sun seeped into her bones, she pulled up her dress and waded in to join them, letting the cool water swirl round her bare legs.

It was very pleasant, though she wished Cain had been one of the fathers who'd come ashore with his children. Not that it mattered a jot to *her,* but it would have been nice for Ben, and would have done Cain good, too. But of course, he was too busy being the genial host and being feted by his peers...and Tiffany.

Eventually they were ferried back to the motor yacht, which was ready to head back. Mardi didn't attempt to join the other guests this time, choosing to follow the boys about as they darted from deck to deck.

Tiffany shot her a supercilious look as they passed by on the stairs, making her uncomfortably aware that her sundress was damp and crumpled and her hair was in need of a good brushing.

Cain found them later on the upper sundeck, where he'd met up with them earlier in the day. "Everything okay?" he asked her, his eyes as shimmering a blue as the water below.

"We're having a great time." And she was—if she didn't pause to think too much.

"Wouldn't you rather be with the women than chasing after these little rascals? I could take them under my wing for a while."

"Thanks, Cain, but I like being with the boys. That's why you invited me," she reminded him. "To keep an eye on them."

"To *help* keep an eye on them. If you'd rather be—"

"I wouldn't. Truly. You go back and join your friends."

He seemed to hesitate for a second, his eyes raking hers for a heart-stopping second. It was a relief when the blue gaze veered away. "Well, don't hesitate to join us if you change your mind."

She forced a smile as he swung on his heel and disappeared down the stairs. He'd given her a pleasant day of freedom on the harbor, as he'd promised, and he'd given her the chance to mingle with the people he worked and socialized with. It wasn't his fault if she hadn't appreciated the day to the full.

But I did enjoy it, Cain, she wanted to call after him. *And the boys did, too. I enjoyed being with them and I enjoyed being with—*

She snapped off the thought before it fully formed in her mind. It wouldn't do to start thinking that way. To start thinking of *him* that way. Tiffany and Sylvia were Cain's type of women, not ordinary, penniless suburban housewives like Mardi Sinclair, the hired cook and baby-sitter. She would never fit into his world, and she would never want to!

Chapter Eight

Cain made a special effort to come home from work early the next day, to have dinner with Ben and to hear about his first day at school. But his son kicked up a fuss because he wanted to have dinner with Nicky. Cain tried to reason with him, pointing out that the two boys saw quite enough of each other as it was and they didn't have to have dinner together every night, as well.

"But I want to eat with *Nicky*," Ben persisted, glaring at his father. Any minute now, Cain knew his son would start stamping his feet and throwing a tantrum.

He tried to stay calm. "We have to let Mardi and her grandfather have Nicky to themselves once in a while, Ben...just as I want to have some time alone with you."

Ben cast a dubious look at his father. "I wish Mardi and Nicky and Grandpa lived with us," he said with a pout.

He was calling Ernie *Grandpa* now? Cain thought of his father, back in New Zealand. Ben could have had a *real* grandfather if Sherman Templar hadn't been such an unreasonable, intolerant jerk. He scowled. It was his father's loss if Ben had turned to Ernie for a grandfather figure.

"They practically do live with us," he reminded his son. "They live in our granny flat. They share the same grounds. They couldn't live any closer."

"They could if they—"

"Ben!" Cain's voice sharpened. "You're having dinner with me tonight, and Mardi's having dinner with her family. You can play with Nicky after dinner—if Mardi says it's okay." His brow creased as he recalled the way Mardi had scuttled off earlier, the moment he'd arrived home.

Mardi was noticeably distant, noticeably cool, for the rest of the week. Cain was surprised at how much that piqued him—well, okay, *hurt* him—as well as puzzled him. It was as if she were deliberately backing away, keeping him at a distance. He hoped it wasn't because she thought of herself as some kind of employee, for heaven's sake, who must keep her place.

Dammit, she had no reason to think that. Their arrangement had been an equal exchange between two widowed parents who'd needed something from each other. Mardi was giving him far more than he was giving her, though. She was giving his son security and love. The love of a mother, the love of a brother, the security of a loving family...things that his son, through no fault of his own, had barely known before. Cain owed her a lot. She'd *taught* him a lot—about himself, about Ben, about his son's special needs. Needs that Cain, caught up in the demanding world of high-powered finance, had neglected without realizing it.

Tiffany, the shrew, had to be responsible for this change in Mardi. She'd treated Mardi like dirt, first on the boat on Sunday and again here at his home a couple of nights ago. She'd bowled in, unannounced, after he'd come home early for the third evening in a row, and Mardi, who'd been preparing Ben's dinner at the time, had let her in.

It still maddened him when he thought of the way Tiffany had treated Mardi, talking down to her as if she were a menial servant rather than the mother of his son's best friend. "The cook showed me in," was how Tiffany had referred to Mardi when he'd come to see who was at his door. *The cook,* he'd noted irately, not *Mardi,* one of the guests he'd invited on board his boat.

He hadn't missed the look of disdain Tiffany had cast Mardi's way before turning back to him, all sweetness and charm, waving some papers under his nose. "You left work before I could give you these papers, Cain. You were going to check them for me. You've been rushing home early a lot this week." Honey flowed from her voice. "It's not like you."

"I'm trying to spend more time with my son." What did Tiffany *think* he'd been doing? "I'm about to have dinner with Ben," he'd told her curtly. "I'll look them over tonight and discuss them with you in the morning."

Tiffany hadn't liked it, but he'd given her no choice but to turn around and leave. She'd gone without even acknowledging Mardi's presence in the kitchen as she'd passed by the open door. If she wasn't so good at her job, he'd tell her to go jump.

Mardi had been so busy all week she'd barely had time to think, which was probably just as well. She hadn't *wanted* to think.

Thinking aroused teasing images of Cain and his glamorous partner Tiffany...of Cain kissing Tiffany...deep, lingering kisses that seared into Mardi's mind, casting a pall over her. Best not to think at all.

Now that the school year was under way, she'd fallen

into a routine, dropping the boys off at St. Mark's each morning, then working all day at the girls' school before picking up the boys in the afternoon and doing any shopping on the way home. Upon arriving home, the first thing she did was to check on Grandpa, who'd been trying all week to hide his pain but was obviously suffering terribly, especially at night.

The steamy summer heat didn't help. Sydney was in the grip of another heat wave, the worst for the summer. It had been too hot even to take Scoots for his usual afternoon run in the park. Instead, she'd urged the big Labrador to cool down under the garden sprinkler, letting the boys join in while she caught up on her household chores. When she had the time to watch the boys more closely, she let them take a dip in Cain's pool, joining them until it was time to start preparing dinner.

She'd been falling into bed exhausted each night. Part of her grinding fatigue, she knew, was due to worry and stress. Worry over her family's health and the constant battle to make ends meet and stress from trying to avoid close contact with Cain. He hadn't made it easy for her to stay aloof, choosing this week of all weeks to come home early each evening, despite his demanding job. While giving him full marks for putting his son ahead of his work for once, she'd found it difficult to avoid him when she had to cook his evening meal and work in his kitchen, and when both of them had to drag their sons apart later in the evening to have their baths and go to bed.

But somehow she'd managed it, fobbing Ben off when he'd demanded, after dining alone with his father for the third night in a row, that Nicky's family join them for dinner the following night.

"Not this week, Ben." She'd stood firm as she'd marched

Nicky back to the granny flat, ignoring Ben's scowls and pouts.

Nicky wasn't happy, either. "*Why* can't we all eat together?" His eyes, behind his purple-rimmed glasses, were pained. "Why can't we all eat together like a family?"

Like a family? Mardi's heart swooped downward. She hardened her heart. Her son would have to face facts. "Because we're *not* a family, Nicky. Ben has his home and you have yours. You have to allow Ben and his father time to be alone, just the two of them. Just as Grandpa and I want to have *you* alone when we can. You see enough of Ben, as it is."

"Ben doesn't *want* to be alone with his father."

Mardi felt a twinge of pity for Cain. His high-powered job and long hours away from home had cast a wedge between him and his son. And though Cain was making an effort, his son didn't want him or appreciate his attempts to bond with him.

"Ben and I want to live in the same house," Nicky grumbled. "We want to be brothers."

"Well, you can't live together and you're not brothers," she snapped. "You'll have to be content with being best friends."

She could feel her stress levels rising. By Friday evening they'd risen to breaking point. Nicky had come home from school that afternoon with a sore throat and smashed glasses, having tripped as he'd rushed out of school. After putting her son to bed and suggesting that Ben play out in the garden with Scoots—she didn't want him catching Nicky's sore throat—she'd called the optician to order another pair of glasses, though heaven knew how she was going to pay for them.

Then she'd checked her mail. There was a letter from the law firm Darrell had worked for, enclosing a bill for a personal purchase Darrell had made on his company's credit card. It was for an amount that made her recoil.

Twenty thousand dollars! She couldn't believe her eyes.

The purchase had been made at Sotheby's, the famous antique dealers.

Darrell had spent twenty thousand dollars at Sotheby's? Her skin crawled. He certainly hadn't bought any antique furniture or jewelry for *her.* Or for himself, as far as she knew.

Her mouth went dry. Had he bought something outrageously expensive for Sylvia Templar?

It had to be a mistake. Mardi searched the phone book for Sotheby's phone number and picked up the phone.

When she hung up a few minutes later her shoulders had slumped. Darrell had bought a rare Lalique vase. She felt sick. And now his law firm expected payment.

Despair washed over her. Where was the vase now? Somewhere in Cain's house, among the other exquisite objets d'art?

Lalique... A faint memory teased her. She'd heard the word only recently. Suddenly she remembered. A crushed box had been found in the wreckage of Darrell's car, with the shattered remains of a glass object, thought to be Lalique glassware.

Darrell must have given it to Sylvia during their illicit weekend in the Blue Mountains. Mardi dropped her head in her hands. How in heaven's name was she going to find an extra twenty thousand dollars?

"Mummy!" The cry came from Nicky's bedroom. Mardi forgot her troubles and rushed to his side. He was burning up with fever. The glands in his neck had become swollen and tender and he had an earache.

She groaned, knowing the signs by now. Tonsillitis

again! Now he would need a doctor...and probably anti-biotics. More expenses!

Mardi wondered if the doctor would put Nicky straight into hospital this time. He'd told her that if Nicky had any further bouts of tonsillitis he'd have to have his tonsils out without delay—meaning that Nicky would shoot to the top of the waiting list instead of having to wait...and wait.

While dreading the thought of Nicky having an operation, she hoped that this time, if it had to happen, it would happen now, quickly, so that her son would soon be fit and healthy again.

But it didn't happen. When the doctor called in later, he told her there was a nurses' strike at the moment and hundreds of beds had been closed in public hospitals, making the wait for a bed even longer and more critical than before. "We'll just have to dose him up and hope for the best."

Mardi nodded mutely, holding her son's hand as the doctor gave her son a jab of antibiotics. "Try to sleep now, munchkin," she said soothingly after the doctor had gone. "I'll be right here." At least she didn't have to cook Cain's dinner tonight. He'd told her this morning that he and Ben had been invited out for dinner this evening. She refused to speculate on who might have issued the invitation.

Cain called in before they left for dinner, with an anxious-looking Ben at his side. "Ben tells me Nicky's not well, Mardi, and that you've had the doctor in."

She cleared her throat, determined that however churned up she felt inside, her voice was going to sound normal. "He has tonsillitis. The doctor gave him an injection."

"That's too bad." Cain frowned. She looked pale and gaunt, he thought, as if all the stuffing had been knocked out of her.

"Are *you* all right?" He heard the sharpness in his tone, but it was too late to modify it.

She jerked her chin upward. "Of course I'm all right." She glowered at him. *I've got other more important things to worry about than the way I look.*

"Nicky will be all right, Mardi." Cain took a step toward her and she quickly stepped back. "The injection should help."

"I know. He'll bounce back in a couple of days." But *would* he? Each bout seemed to be worse and lasted longer than the previous one. Mardi realized she was breathing too fast and made an effort to slow it down. She didn't want Cain probing any deeper. She turned to Ben and forced a smile, but it wavered.

"Is there anything I can do?" Cain asked. She could feel his eyes burning into her face, delving below the fragile surface calm, threatening to strip away the last shred of her composure.

Yes, you can go...just go. "No...thank you." It was an effort to speak. "Nicky's sleeping at the moment." She couldn't look at him. "Cain, I've a hundred things to do...."

"Of course you have. Sorry, Mardi. Look, we won't be late home if you do think of anything we can—"

"We'll be fine. Have a good night." She directed the comment to Ben, not his father.

She leaned against the door for a few seconds after she'd closed it behind them, taking several deep, gulping breaths. She simply had to pull herself together. If she fell into a heap, what would Nicky and Grandpa do then?

But how was she going to get out of this latest appalling mess?

Mardi couldn't sleep. It was the early hours of the morning and she'd been up several times in the night to check on Nicky and to see what she could do for Grandpa when she heard him moaning in his bed. She'd given him some more painkillers and a soothing hip rub, but they barely helped anymore. It killed her to see him in so much pain.

She lay wide-awake in her hot, rumpled bed, cursing her heartless husband for letting their private health insurance lapse, cursing him for plunging his family into such crippling debt, cursing him for falling for Sylvia Templar and ruining all their lives.

It wasn't fair. With the amount of money Darrell had spent on that vase, she could have paid for Nicky's operation at a private hospital, and maybe even Grandpa's, too. *What was she going to do?*

She gave up trying to sleep and hauled herself out of bed. Pulling on her swimsuit, she grabbed a towel, found her set of keys and slipped out of the granny flat. Nicky's window was wide open and she would hear if he happened to call out for her, and Scoots was at the foot of his bed— she'd brought him inside at Nicky's request—ready to bark if the boy woke again.

Moments later she'd unlocked the pool gate and was teetering at the edge of the pool, which was bathed in soft, pearly moonlight. She hesitated for only a second before taking a long deep breath and diving into the deep end of the pool.

Bliss! It felt so good she didn't want to come up; she just wanted to feel the cool water flowing over her heated body, caressing her skin, cooling her cheeks and tightly closed eyes, and streaming through her hair like soothing fingers.

Like a man's soothing fingers…

Soothing fingers that suddenly changed to a vice-like grip. Someone was dragging her through the water! She could feel a hard bare chest clamped up against her back, firm thighs tangling with her flailing legs, strong arms holding her in an iron grasp. She gasped for air as her head broke the surface. Drawing all her strength, she began to struggle.

"Let me go!"

"No way!" The deep voice was close to a snarl. "Just keep still!"

It was *Cain's* voice.

"What do you think you're doing?" she squawked, horrified at the way her body was responding to the sensuous feel of his, despite the far from gentle grip of his arms and the almost frightening roughness of his voice.

"Stopping you from doing something stupid," came the incomprehensible reply.

She looked up at him dazedly—*What was stupid about going for a midnight swim?*—as he dragged her up the pool steps and lowered her onto the hard ceramic tiles. But he didn't let her go. Still clasping her round the waist, he dropped to his knees, a hand shooting out to snatch up her towel. Only then did he draw back far enough to wrap it around her, but he gathered her back into his arms, cradling her against him.

She turned her head, hazarding a look up at him. But he was the one who spoke first.

"You gave me one hell of a fright," he growled, his dark brows slanted low over the silvery gleam of his eyes, his powerful shoulders hunched over her, gleaming wet in the soft moonlight.

"You—you thought I was an intruder?" she whispered, wondering dimly why she was no longer trying to struggle out of his arms. This was madness. He was practically naked!

Almost of their own volition, her eyes flickered downward, but all she could see were his powerful thighs, well-muscled calves and bare feet. Her towel-clad body—mercifully perhaps—hid the rest of him.

'No, I didn't think you were an intruder.'' He shifted slightly, as if her closeness was making him uncomfortable.

Mardi's skin prickled. Was it just a spontaneous masculine reaction she felt? Or did he...actually *want* her, feel a strong physical *desire* for her?

This is Cain Templar, she reminded herself with a twinge of bitterness, and a faint pang at the same time. He wouldn't want her any more than she would want him. She tried to wriggle out of his arms.

"No, you don't.'' His grip tightened, bringing her dangerously close again. "I saw you from the upstairs balcony. I hadn't been able to sleep and I'd come outside for a breath of air. When I saw you heading for the pool I decided to join you.''

"But you *didn't* join me for a swim,'' she accused, lamenting the unsteadiness she could hear in her voice. "You hauled me out of the pool as if—as if you didn't think I should be there. Yet, you lent me a key to your pool and said we could use it any time we liked.''

"I remember only too well.'' His voice roughened. "I regretted being so trusting when I saw you dive into the pool and not come up.''

"You mean you thought I was drowning and jumped in to *save* me?''

His brow lowered farther. "Silly of me, wasn't it—when you obviously didn't *want* to be saved. Or have you changed your mind now? Have you realized what it would have done to your son and your grandfather if you'd drowned yourself—and to Ben and me, too?''

She stared up at him, her head whirling. "What are you talking about?'' It was a broken whisper. "You...think I was trying to—''

"Well, weren't you?" He forced her chin up, his eyes piercing hers, his scorn flaying her. "I saw the state you were in earlier this evening. There's obviously something wrong. If it's something you couldn't handle, why the hell didn't you come to me?"

Mardi didn't know whether to laugh or cry. Hysterical laughter, hysterical tears. Somehow she managed not to give way to either.

"Cain, stop—please! I wasn't trying to drown myself. I just wanted to cool down, that's all. I—I'm sorry if I scared you."

Scared him? Cain's mouth twisted. It had made him angry. Damned angry. Why *was* he so angry? Why had he said, "Think what it would have done to Ben and *me*," as if he *cared?* Why had he imagined she would come to *him* with her problems?

He relaxed his grip. "And I'm sorry if I overreacted." He didn't understand it. Cain Templar rarely overreacted. He rarely cared enough. Caring made a man vulnerable.

And why the hell was he still *holding* her? It was playing havoc with his senses. With more than his senses. He wondered at the heat racing through his body, the fire heating his loins.

The reaction was totally unexpected. He'd had only one thought in his mind when he'd jumped into the pool—the burning need to save her. Now *he* was burning, the feel of her soft skin stirring feelings that, though familiar, somehow *weren't* familiar.

It's pure animal lust, you fool. It only felt different, he reasoned, because *she* was different, unlike other women he'd known. Unlike Sylvia, who'd once fired his blood, too—only, not like this. Not with this painful, aching tenderness, a feeling alien to him.

Mardi had given him a fright; that was all it was.

But *something* was seriously wrong, seriously worrying her. He'd sensed it earlier, and he hadn't been able to think of anything else all evening. It was why he hadn't been able to sleep.

He had to find out what was wrong. But he'd have to be careful how he went about it. He frowned in thought, then approached it from left field.

"Ben tells me Nicky didn't join in his swimming class after school the other day. He stayed with you." He cocked an eyebrow at her.

It took a moment for Mardi to follow his change of tack. When his words sank in, she glanced warily up at him, noting the raised eyebrow. *As if he knew...*

"Nicky's had a sore throat," she hedged, determined not to admit that she could no longer afford his lessons.

"Not on Wednesday, he didn't," Cain said, and felt her tense in his arms. "He was well enough to paddle around in the toddlers' pool, Ben said."

"Yeah, well, I was just taking precautions—not wanting him to get overtired." Mardi jutted her chin. "And now that he *is* sick, he won't be going swimming again for quite a while." *Or having his infected tonsils removed, either, thanks to Darrell.* Unwanted tears welled in her eyes. She blinked them away.

Suddenly conscious that she was still in his arms, she croaked, "I'd better get back inside. Nicky might be calling for me." She wrenched herself free and rose unsteadily to her feet.

Chapter Nine

"Mardi, you can't fight this alone...whatever it is." Cain's voice was low and seductively gentle. "You must trust me."

Mardi's body quivered in a surge of longing. How she wished she *could* trust him. "I've found it better to rely on myself rather than other people," she said coldly.

"Try me." His brows were drawn, his eyes shadowed in the soft moonlight. He was leading her away from the pool as he spoke, through the gate onto the soft lawn behind, where he swung her round to face him. "It's Nicky and Ernie, isn't it? You're worried sick because they both need operations and nothing's happening. You're getting desperate because you feel you can't do anything about it." His gaze pinned hers.

Mardi felt a rising anger. Cain wouldn't understand desperation...a man with his millions. And it wasn't just Nicky and Grandpa...it was this latest horrendous debt, coming just when she thought there couldn't be any more. She began to shake.

"There's more to it than Nicky and your grandfather
isn't there?" Cain's eyes bored into hers, demanding the
truth. "You're in serious financial difficulties…. That's
what's worrying you half to death, am I right?" He held
up a hand as her eyes flew to his. "I know you won't say
a word against your husband, Mardi. You obviously loved
him, despite what he—"

"How could you possibly know how I felt about my
husband?" Her voice sliced over his, her body shaking with
rage. Cain assumed that she was protecting her husband out
of *love* for him, when all she felt for him was loathing and
disgust. She was damned if she was going to let Cain go
on believing such a fairy tale, and pitying her. It was *Nicky*
she'd been trying to protect, not her faithless, grasping husband.

"My husband killed any love I had for him long
ago…even before he met your wife." The bitter truth
spilled out. "But Nicky loved his father, and he believes
Darrell loved and cared for *him,* and I don't want that to
change. So if you ever tell my son—"

"I won't breathe a word, I promise." Cain assured her,
lowering his eyelids to hide a gleam of triumph. So, she'd
been protecting her son, not her husband's memory. Good,
he thought with satisfaction. "He left you with serious
debts?" he asked gently.

Mardi thought of denying it, of keeping up the facade
that Darrell had cared about his family, but she found herself nodding, relieved to have the burden of bitter knowledge off her chest. *A problem shared,* Cain had said once.
Cain was a financial whiz, an experienced man of the
world. He might know of some legal loophole that would
relieve her of the responsibility of Darrell's debts.

But she didn't really believe it, knowing she was clutch-
ing at straws. She felt a twinge of pity for Cain, wondering

ust how much he'd cared for his beautiful, unfaithful wife.
Cold and unemotional as he appeared on the surface, he
wasn't a completely unfeeling man, or he wouldn't be so
concerned about Nicky and Grandpa. Or her.

Cain watched her changing expressions. It was clear now
that Mardi hadn't left her home because it held lingering
memories of her husband, as he'd assumed…. She'd left
because she could no longer afford to keep it. For the same
reason she'd almost taken Nicky out of St. Mark's. Her
irresponsible husband was to blame for everything that had
happened to her. His hands clenched into fists.

He'd long suspected she was in serious trouble financially. It was the reason he'd secretly paid Nicky's school
fees—in strictest confidence, of course. He'd known Mardi
would never knowingly accept any financial help from him.

But now, maybe, she would agree to let him help her.
But there might be only one way to persuade her….

He felt his heartbeat quicken, the way it did when he
was on the verge of a challenging merger. He'd made snap
decisions in the past, and he hadn't regretted them. Now
he was about to make another—maybe the biggest gamble
of his life—and he profoundly hoped he wouldn't live to
regret this one.

"Mardi…" He lowered his voice, wanting her to think
of him more as a friend than a high-handed benefactor. "I
know you'd do anything for your son and your grandfather.
But I can help. Nicky and Ernie could have their operations
tomorrow if—"

"If I accepted charity from you?" Mardi injected scorn
into her voice to hide the pain and uncertainty she felt at
having to refuse his offer. Would Nicky and Grandpa understand her high moral stand? Was she being fair to *them*?

"Nicky's become like a second son to me, Mardi. It
wouldn't be charity if he was my son…legally."

Mardi jerked back. "You want to adopt my son and take him away from me?" Outrage brought a tremor to her voice. "You're that desperate to keep Nicky and Ben together?"

"No, Mardi! No, of course not. I'd never take your son away from you. I'm just saying I could look after Nicky if he was my son."

She pierced him with a molten glare. "But he's not your son."

"He would be if you were my wife and I legally adopted him."

His *wife!* He was joking.... He had to be. "I have no intention of getting married again," she said with a valiant attempt at dignity. "Or even getting involved with anyone again."

"I feel the same," Cain said coolly. "But I'm not talking about emotional involvement, Mardi. I'm talking about a practical partnership for the sake of our sons. I want a mother for Benjamin, and you're the mother he wants. You care for him, don't you?"

"You know I do." Her eyes misted a little. She cared too much. "But—"

"And Nicky needs a father and financial security. And I—" Cain paused, his eyes seeming to caress her for a second, making her pulses leap. "I need a wife. A wife who will be a companion, a homemaker, a hostess when I entertain and a partner at business functions."

He *needed* a wife, not *wanted* a wife, Mardi noted. Well, *she* had no wish for emotional involvement, either. But a practical, cold-blooded marriage? She shivered.

"If it's a business companion and social hostess you want, why not ask your friend Tiffany?" The caustic question leapt out. "She'd make a perfect corporate wife."

"Tiffany?" The edge of Cain's mouth looped slightly.

"Tiffany's not the homemaking, settling-down type. Or the motherly type."

No, she's the femme fatale type, Mardi thought. The type a man has an affair with. As Cain would no doubt continue to do after marrying the motherly, homemaking type. As he saw *her*.

"This whole idea's crazy—"

"You think it's crazy to give our sons new parents who care for them, a new family, stability? You think it's crazy to give Nicky and Ernie the chance to have their operations at the best private hospitals, with the best surgeons? You think it's crazy to marry a man who's willing to settle all your debts and give your family financial security in the future? Naturally, as your husband, I'd be responsible for any debts you've incurred."

"They're not *my* debts," she fired back, pride flaring for a spirited second. "I wouldn't *be* in debt if my husband hadn't put me in this impossible position!" She raised her chin. "I'm earning a perfectly good salary, and I could have supported my son, and Grandpa, too, if I hadn't had those horrendous debts thrust on me."

She slumped a little. The reality was, she *did* have debts and she had no hope of helping her ailing family in the foreseeable future. And their needs had to come before anything.

"I know that, Mardi. I know you're a responsible person. It's one of the things I admire most about you." Cain's hands moved up her arms to close over her shoulders. "Mardi, say yes. The boys are like brothers already. Brothers and best friends. They want to be together as a family."

She couldn't dispute that. But *marriage?* "Cain, you don't have to marry me to help me." Her voice wobbled. It wasn't easy to back down. "If you seriously want to help Nicky and Grandpa I'll accept a loan—just to cover their operations. But heaven knows when I'll be able to pay you back.''

Cain shook his head. "My offer stands. It's marriage or nothing. Then we all benefit. Ben and I,'' he said, spelling it out, "need you as much as you need us.'' He couldn't believe the words were coming out of his mouth. She'd offered him a way out—agreeing to accept a conditional loan, against all her principles—and he'd refused to take it!

"It would never work,'' she argued. She still believed that marriage, to work successfully, should be based on love...or at least on mutual caring. "Marriage is more than...cold practicalities.''

"I agree with you,'' Cain said. And he bent his head and kissed her.

The touch of his lips sent instant fire through her, and a languorous weakness. Far from repulsing her, or leaving her cold, the searing, all-too-real kiss sent her senses reeling. She felt her lips responding, melting under his in a torrent of new and exquisite sensations. Why had Darrell's kisses never felt like this?

Her breath quickened as she strained into him. She felt his hands slide up her body, his palms hot on her skin. For a wild moment she wanted him to drag her down onto the grass and fuse her body to his.

Cain was rocked by a sudden rush of desire so strong it nearly sent him over the edge. He lifted his head and let his hands drop away. His breath was uneven, his eyes a dark glitter in the fading moonlight. "You see? There's fire between us, there's chemistry. That's more than a lot of couples have.'' His voice was strangely hoarse. Dammit, he'd never expected to feel... *What had he felt?*

All he knew was that if he'd let it go on a moment longer, he would have been in danger of losing control, and maybe scaring her off with the scorching heat of his passion.

The idea of Cain Templar losing control almost made him laugh aloud. He never lost control. He'd always been in full control of his emotions and his hormones. He'd never known or understood emotional involvement, not even at the height of his passion for Sylvia. He wasn't the emotional type.

Mardi sagged in his arms, her lips moist and swollen, her head still whirling, even as cold reality doused the flames inside her. Fire. Chemistry. *Sex.* Yes, but not love, not emotion. No, he'd made that clear. Could she live with that?

Mardi had married with her heart before—and look where it had led her. She didn't want to go through that emotional turmoil again—the hurt, the disillusionment. Best not to have an emotional involvement at all.

Cain was being straight with her, and forewarned was forearmed. Mardi lifted her chin. If she didn't allow herself to fall in love with him, which was hardly a danger, maybe they could make it work. For the sake of their sons.

Having Ben for a brother and a best friend would enhance Nicky's life and give him a feeling of belonging, and having Cain for a father would give her son the security that she couldn't provide, much as she had tried to.

And there was Grandpa.... He'd be looked after, too. He'd be able to move around again, once he'd had his hip operation.

"Over the weekend I'll give you the name of the best surgeon for Nicky and the best orthopedic surgeon for Ernie." Cain's voice wove seductively through her musings. "On Monday you can get referrals from your local doctor and arrange for Ernie to have his operation as soon as possible, and Nicky, too, when he's over this bout of tonsillitis.

As for your husband's debts, Mardi, settling them will be my wedding present to you."

He paused, looking down at her with an expression she couldn't read. She hoped her own thoughts were as well masked. "All you have to say is yes, Mardi, and I'll put the wheels into motion. A month's notice is required, so you'll have four weeks to concentrate on Nicky's and Ernie's operations before we tie the knot."

Mardi gulped. All she had to do was say yes…and all her worries would be over.

There was no choice to make. Nicky and Grandpa came first and always would. "All right, yes," she said, her voice squeaking a little on the word that was going to change her life forever.

"You've made the right decision." He kissed her again—a brief brush of his lips this time, as if to seal their deal—before stepping aside. "Now, off you go and get some sleep."

Sleep? Mardi felt a rising bubble of hysteria, wondering if she was sealing a deal or sealing her *fate*. She slipped past him and ran.

Cain stayed where he was for a few seconds longer, watching her slender figure fade into the gloom.

Whether this morning was going to be good or bad for either of them, only time would tell. The only thing he was sure of was that their sons would be over the moon.

Chapter Ten

They decided not to tell the boys, or anyone else, until after Nicky and Grandpa had had their operations. Cain sensed that Mardi wouldn't want any distractions taking her mind off her family, and there was bound to be gossip after what had happened between their spouses. They could both do without that right now. No one need know until after they were married—in a month's time.

On Tuesday, Sydney's top orthopedic surgeon saw Grandpa and arranged for him to have his hip operation at a private hospital on Friday morning of that same week. On Thursday, Mardi took Nicky to see a highly qualified surgeon, who agreed to remove his infected tonsils the following Wednesday.

With so much happening, Mardi resigned from her job at the girls' school. She would have needed to take off too much time over the next few weeks.

"You'll have no trouble finding another job if you decide later that you want one," Cain consoled her when she told him. "You're an intelligent, well-educated, multiskilled woman, Mardi. Not that you'll need to work, once we're married,'' he reminded her. "It'll only be if you want to.''

No, she thought with a faint pang, I won't *need* to work. I'll have a rich husband to support me. Cain had already arranged for her to have her own checkbook linked to his bank account, and without even asking to examine her debts first, had insisted she pay off the lot immediately. He trusted her, even though they weren't yet husband and wife. And he trusted her not to abuse his trust.

It was a strange feeling, being trusted with a man's money. While taking one load off her shoulders, it added another. It didn't feel right. It made her feel guilty, inadequate, inept, as well as totally dependent on him. She *would* get another job, she decided, once she'd settled into her new life.

She didn't want an all-consuming, full-time career. She'd long ago given up the idea of resuming her library training and becoming a librarian. It would have to be a part-time job that would fit in with her growing family.

Friday came quickly. Grandpa had been admitted to the hospital the night before.

Mardi spent the morning waiting by the phone. The surgeon had promised to call her immediately after Ernie's operation. It was the longest morning she'd ever endured and she felt tears squeezing from her eyes. What if something had gone wrong?

At last the phone rang. She snatched it up, her heart in her mouth. "Mardi Sinclair." It was a breathless whisper.

"Mardi, it's me, Cain. Heard anything yet?''

She couldn't speak for a second, too choked up with emotion. "Not yet," she finally managed to answer, and heard the fraught note in her voice.

"Mardi, just hold on. I'll be right over.''

He was coming home? She replaced the phone and

pressed her palms to her chest. She wasn't sure she wanted him here. Since last Friday night he'd kept his distance physically, not even touching her, but the sexual tension between them had been palpable.

By the time the front doorbell rang she'd shredded a box of tissues and most of her fingernails, as well. "Come in. The door's not locked." She was afraid that if she went to the door she might weaken and fall into Cain's arms the moment she saw him. Safer to stay by the phone.

He strode in, his blue business shirt unbuttoned at the throat, his tie loosened.

"Still no news?" Stupid question, Cain thought. She wouldn't be watching the phone the way she was if she'd heard. He noted the pieces of tissue on the carpet and felt an odd tug at his gut. He hadn't been around people who cared about their families the way Mardi did.

He saw her slump into an armchair, which prevented him from grabbing her in his arms, as he was tempted to do. But he'd already decided on a strategic retreat in that volatile area. He wanted Mardi safely married to him before he unleashed his passion on her.

And besides, he wanted all her worries to be over, and all her attention to be on him, when she came to his bed.

He wasn't sure where this newfound delicacy of feeling had come from, or why he didn't just take what he wanted, the way he always had in the past. He only knew that it was different with Mardi and that her feelings mattered to him. Maybe even more than his own, because she had more feeling and humanity for other people than he did.

Some of her sensitivity was even beginning to rub off on him. He'd become much closer to his son since Mardi had come into their lives. She'd *taught* him to care more, to give more of himself, to enjoy his son, rather than holding himself aloof, the way he always had before.

"I'll wait with you," he said, and sat down in the opposite armchair, burying a twinge of regret. His fingers still itched to run through her hair and over her skin, but they'd just have to go on itching for a while longer. Her mind and heart were elsewhere right now, and her family deserved her full attention.

The phone startled her and she fumbled with it before clamping it to her ear. "Yes? It's Mardi Sinclair here."

Cain watched her face, saw the dawning relief, the joyful tears gather in her eyes, blurring the clear hazel.

"Oh, thank you, Doctor, thank you. Oh, can I? Yes, yes, I'll be in right away." Her eyes were shining as she turned to face him. "The operation was a complete success. He's awake, and they say I can come in and see him if I like. Just for a few minutes."

"I'll take you." Cain jumped up. "I'll drop you off at the hospital and wait for you. Then we'll grab a bite to eat, and by then it should be time to pick up the boys from school. How about I cook a barbecue tea and throw a salad together this evening to save you having to do anything yourself? If you want to go back to the hospital afterward, I'll be home all evening to look after the boys. Nicky can sleep in Ben's room."

She met his eyes. "You're taking the rest of the day off?"

"They can contact me on my cell phone or at home if they need me. Today's Ernie's day. I'm glad everything went well, Mardi."

She realized her eyes were clinging to his, mesmerized by the warmth she saw in the glittering blue, and she hastily plucked her gaze away, afraid she might be showing too much emotion. *No emotional involvement,* he'd said.

"Yes, I'm so relieved," she admitted, blinking rapidly

as she turned away. "I just hope Nicky's operation is as successful."

"It will be, Mardi. Robert Cunningham is the best surgeon he could have, and he's done this operation hundreds of times." It took sheer force of will for Cain to refrain from putting an arm round her shoulders as they left the house.

First thing Wednesday morning, Mardi and Ben, who'd insisted on coming, too, took Nicky to the same private hospital that Grandpa was in, staying with him until he was ready to be wheeled into the operating theater. He looked so small and vulnerable in his hospital gown and cap that Mardi's heart squeezed in her chest. But she forced a bright smile.

"You're going to be fine, munchkin," she whispered as she gave him a final kiss. Ben bent and gave Nicky a peck, too, his blue eyes huge and dark under his fringe of silky hair. Overawed at the thought of what was about to happen to his beloved friend, Ben's usual cheeky confidence was nowhere in sight.

"See ya, mate."

"See ya, mate," Nicky echoed as he was whisked away.

Mardi slipped an arm round Ben's shoulders—wishing, in that moment, that she had someone to put an arm around *her*. But Grandpa was on a different floor of the hospital, and Cain had gone to an early-morning board meeting, which he'd said he couldn't avoid.

"Come on, tiger," she said to Ben, "I'll take you to school."

"Why can't I wait here with you?" Ben cast an entreating look up at her.

"Because we could have a long wait, and Nicky won't be well enough to talk for a while."

The surgeon had assured her it was a simple procedure that he'd done many times before, but he'd been obliged to point out the possible dangers, too, and she was frighteningly aware that even the best surgeons could make mistakes at times.

After dropping off Ben at the school, she drove straight back to the hospital and settled down—or tried to—in the waiting area near the operating room. She tried to think positively—to think of Grandpa, who was making slow but steady progress after his own far more serious operation. He was already hobbling around the ward.

His doctor had told her that Ernie would be in the hospital for another week at least, before being shifted to the rehabilitation wing for a further couple of weeks. But he was improving each day—she could see that for herself—and each day her heart lightened a little more.

She glanced anxiously at her watch. Every minute seemed like an hour. She jumped up and began to pace, gripping her hands tensely against her chest.

"I take it he's still in there?" said a familiar deep voice from behind.

"Oh, Cain!" It was such a relief to see him, to have someone to share this endless waiting with, someone to talk to, that she almost threw herself at him. Almost. "It's taking much longer than they said it would." Her voice shook. "I'm scared to death."

"Robert Cunningham never rushes his operations," Cain soothed, his presence, Mardi noticed, drawing the interested eyes of everyone within range. And no wonder, she thought, diverted for a merciful second. All the other people waiting, including herself, were dressed casually, even sloppily, while Cain was the epitome of suave masculine elegance in his classic business suit and red silk tie, his piercing blue eyes and impressive bearing making him stand out even more.

"I can't stand this waiting!" The strangled cry wrenched from her. "I—I just couldn't bear it if anything happened to Nicky."

"I know." Cain could feel her pain—which startled him for a second. When had he felt anyone's pain before? "But nothing will happen, Mardi." He drew her over to a quiet corner and urged her to sit down, lowering himself into the seat beside her.

"Your board meeting's finished already?" she asked, making an effort to take her mind off Nicky's operation.

"It was dragging on a bit, so I left," he said with a shrug.

He'd left his important board meeting *early?* Mardi looked at him in amazement. For a high-powered merchant banker and self-professed workaholic, this was incredible.

"Mrs. Sinclair?"

She jerked her head around to see a man in a pale green theater gown and cap striding toward them. It was Nicky's surgeon. She jumped up, the blood draining from her face. "Is everything all right?" Her voice was a pathetic croak. She hardly realized she was gripping Cain's arm.

"Your son has come through beautifully, Mrs. Sinclair. He had a bit of bleeding, but we've dealt with that. He'll be a bit sore for a while, but that's to be expected."

She sagged against Cain, relief mingling with sympathy for poor Nicky, wishing she could feel his discomfort for him. "Can I see him?"

"He'll be coming out of recovery shortly. When they wheel him back to his ward, you can stay with him, if you like. He'll need to lie on his side for a while to make sure he doesn't have any more bleeding, but that's just a precaution. He'll be a new boy once his sore throat heals. Children bounce back very quickly." He strode off, throw-

ing over his shoulder, "I'll be back to see him this eve
ning."

She felt Cain's hand covering hers, warmth seeping into
her skin.

"I'm glad everything went well, Mardi. I know how
worried you've been. About Ernie, too."

"And I have you to thank." How could she ever repay
him?

"Now I don't want to hear that kind of talk." Cain's
voice roughened. "We're partners, remember. Nicky's going to be my son, and Ben's going to be yours. It's equal
give and take where you and I are concerned."

She wondered if his friends and colleagues would think
so. The penniless cook marrying the millionaire merchant
banker. The hired baby-sitter becoming mother to his son.
The spurned widow moving into his fine home and into his
bed.

She felt a prickle of apprehension at the thought of sharing Cain's bed.

"I'd better get back to work." Cain's hand touched her
shoulder briefly, then dropped away. "I'll pick up Ben after
school, Mardi, and take him to his swimming lesson. And
I'll let him know that Nicky's okay."

She looked up at him gratefully. He intended to leave
work early *again!* Wings would be sprouting next.
"Thanks. I'll be home in time to cook your dinner—"

"No need for that. I'll bring home some Chinese take-
away. You'll want to get back to the hospital early this
evening, I imagine, to see Nicky. You'll see Ernie, too?"

"If I can leave Nicky for a while this afternoon, I'll pop
up and see Grandpa then. I'll bring Ben in tonight to see
Nicky…if Nicky's up to it." Ben had been so anxious
about the operation this morning, it might reassure him to
see Nicky for himself, even if only briefly.

"Well, only if he's up to it." Cain let his eyes dwell for a moment on her upturned face. *Despite all her worries, she's thinking of others again...of Ben...of Nicky...of Ernie...of what it would mean to the boys to see each other again as soon as possible. When does she ever think of herself?* He'd rarely been around women who felt more concern for other people than they did for themselves.

"Tell Nicky I'll see him in the morning," he said as he left her.

Mardi's eyes followed him. He'd almost looked as if he wanted to stay and see Nicky *now,* with her. But he was thoughtfully letting her see him alone.

Somehow she didn't feel so alone after he'd left.

"Well, how is he?" Cain asked when she arrived home.

"Is Nicky all right?" Ben ran to her, his small face upturned, blue eyes wide.

"He's feeling pretty sore, and he's been on strong pain-killers since the anesthetic wore off, but he's all right— yes." She bent and gave Ben a hug, her eyes misting. "He's anxious to see you, Ben. Would you like to come to the hospital with me tonight? I'm afraid it'll have to be a short visit and he won't feel much like talking, but if you'd like to see him..."

"I would!" He looked up at his father. "Can I, Dad?"

Cain gave his son a smile that softened the hard lines of his face and sent a wave of warmth through Mardi. If only he'd smile more often! If only he'd smile like that for *her.*

But loving smiles weren't part of their deal. Loving anything.

No sooner had they sat down to eat their Chinese food than Cain's cell phone rang. He flicked a switch and held the phone to his ear. "Ah, yes...just a minute, will you?"

He rose from his chair. "I'll take it in my study," he told Mardi, as if it was a call he didn't want her to overhear.

He wanted to talk privately. She thought immediately of Tiffany, and felt a sinking sensation. Or was this a business call and he simply wanted to concentrate, or to refer to some notes in his study?

"I'll put your dinner back in the oven," she called after him as he headed for the door.

Barely a minute after he'd gone the front doorbell rang.

"I'll get it." Ben jumped up and made a dive for the hall.

"Wait, Ben..." She ran after him, catching up as he opened the door...to Tiffany! Tiffany, in a figure-hugging black power suit and impossibly high heels, her black hair tumbling in gleaming waves over her padded shoulders.

When she saw Mardi, her dark eyes flashed with a look of pure malevolence, her scarlet lips curling. "You again!" The blistering contempt in her voice shook Mardi. She could feel the dark eyes raking her face like invisible claws. "You're here to baby-sit? Cain's not at home?" The questions cracked out.

Ben stepped between them. "Mardi's here for dinner," he said, a gloating note in his voice.

Mardi held her breath.

"You're eating *together* now?" The withering scorn in Tiffany's voice cut through the air like a scythe. "Well, you haven't wasted any time, have you?" The dark eyes narrowed, glinting with malice. "So you're the reason he's been taking so much time off. You realize you and your family are dragging him down," she accused Mardi. "He's lost billion-dollar contracts because of you."

Shaken as she was, Mardi tried not to show any reaction. "I'll take you into the lounge. Cain's on the phone at the moment. Ben, go back and finish your dinner."

She led the way along the sweeping marble passage and waved Tiffany into one of the pristine white rooms. As she turned away, Tiffany's vitriol scorched into the air behind her.

"You won't land him, if that's what you're hoping for. You think he'd get tied up with an insipid nobody who *cooks* for him? He likes women with a bit of glamour and sex appeal. And I should know…"

Mardi shut her ears, but the poison was already injected. So they *were* having an affair.

Why, if they were so close, hadn't Cain told Tiffany that he was, in fact, intending to marry the insipid nobody who cooked for him? Mardi found she couldn't eat another mouthful when she rejoined Ben at the table. He'd already finished his own dinner and was gulping down the remains of his glass of flavored milk.

"Go and wash your hands and grab a coat, Ben," she said, trying to steady her voice. "I think we might go…. Your dad could be a while." Cain would know where they'd gone.

The thought of facing him again just now, especially if he had Tiffany in tow, was more than she could bear.

When she and Ben came home later in the evening, Cain was waiting for them. Tiffany, thankfully, had gone.

Involuntarily her gaze flew to his open-necked collar for signs of lipstick, and to his hair for signs of ruffling by fevered fingers, but of course, he would hardly be that careless.

The weight in her stomach felt even heavier than before.

"How was he?" Cain asked, frowning slightly. She looked pretty knocked around herself, even worse than she'd looked earlier in the day as they'd waited to hear the outcome of her son's operation. "Has Nicky had a set-back?"

"No, they say he's coming along fine."

"But he doesn't look too good," Ben piped up with boyish relish. "And he can hardly talk. Mardi's going to take me to see him again tomorrow after school. She says he might be feeling more better by then."

"I'm sure he will." Cain nodded absently. "Ben, why don't you run upstairs and get ready for bed?"

"Can Mardi sleep at our house?" Ben looked up at his father with his most beseeching look. "She'll be all alone without Nicky and Grandpa."

Mardi felt a horrified flutter. "I won't be far away, Ben," she said swiftly, realizing with a flare of heat that Ben was right—she *would* be all alone in her flat tonight. She wished for a brief, poignant moment that things had been different...that she and her husband-to-be were getting married because they loved and wanted each other.

But of course this wasn't a love match. It was a practical, loveless partnership, and although there might be sexual attraction between them, emotion didn't come into it.

As she bid them both good-night and turned to go, Cain caught her arm. "Before you go—" he waved Ben off "—I have something to tell you."

Her insides lurched. "Yes?"

"I'm afraid I have to go away again, just for a few days."

Her spirits plummeted. With Tiffany, did he mean? Of course he did.

"You'll be going interstate?" she asked, retaining her composure with an effort. "Or do you mean overseas?" High-powered merchant bankers often went overseas for just a few days.

"No, no, just into the country. Hunter Valley. There's a

winery there that wants to go public. I'm going there to assess it.''

The state's premier wine district... How nice, she thought. "And you want me to look after Ben?" Poor Ben, she thought. Would he mind his father leaving him again?

"Would you mind, Mardi? I know you have a lot on your plate at the moment with both Nicky and Ernie in hospital—"

"Ben will be at school during the day," she said, "and he can come with me to the hospital after school and maybe in the evening, too." She chewed on her lip. "It'll be a bit more tricky when Nicky comes home. I won't be able to leave him at home alone while I run Ben to school and pick him up again, and go to visit Grandpa." She would have to find a baby-sitter—somehow.

"I'll be back by then," Cain said, "and able to help out."

"Fine," Mardi said. But why *did* this trip bother her so much? It wasn't as if she loved Cain. It wasn't as if Cain was even pretending to love her. *No emotional involvement,* they'd both agreed.

But Cain hadn't specified having no emotional involvement with anyone else.

Chapter Eleven

Two days before their planned wedding day, she met Cain in town to choose a wedding ring. When he asked her to select an engagement ring, as well, she shook her head. "I don't need an engagement ring."

"Then a dress ring," he insisted. "Pick out something you like. A diamond, a sapphire, whatever appeals to you." He'd never known a woman to turn down an offer of jewelry. But Mardi, he had to remember, wasn't like other women. She was funny about him lavishing gifts or spending money on her.

"Please, Cain, I'd rather not. Later on, maybe." She smiled to soften the refusal. But he knew that her smile hid a will of iron. She wasn't going to change her mind.

"As you wish." He paused, then said, "Since we won't be having a honeymoon, we'll take a trip somewhere over the next school holidays, if Ernie and Nicky are up to it. Where would you like to go? To one of the islands? To the Gold Coast? To Disneyland?"

It sounded blissful. She thought for a moment and the

answer came to her. She spoke up before she could change her mind. "I'd like to take the boys to New Zealand."

Cain's face tightened. "Why New Zealand?"

"I'd like to meet your father." Her eyes challenged him. She gulped in a fortifying breath, hoping she wasn't making a big mistake in forcing him to confront a situation she knew nothing about. "Families mean too much, Cain, to give up on them. Especially when they grow old and won't be around forever. Nicky adores his grandpa. I'd like Ben and his grandfather to have the chance to know each other."

"I gave my father that chance." Cain's eyes were wintry, his tone steel edged.

"Did you, Cain?" Mardi spoke gently. "Or did you give up too easily—without giving it a chance?" She wondered where she'd found the strength to stand up to Cain.

His lips drew tight. How had she come to know him so well? He *had* stormed off without even trying to bring his father around. But *he* knew how pigheaded and stubborn his old man was. *She* didn't.

"Give him another chance, Cain." Mardi's soft voice persisted. "For all your sakes. Especially for Ben's."

To refuse would make him as stubborn and pigheaded as his father. And maybe he was. Maybe that had been the trouble all along. "I guess everyone deserves a second chance," he conceded.

The next morning Grandpa collapsed. One minute he was sitting at the kitchen table drinking his morning coffee, the next he lay slumped over the table.

"Grandpa, what's wrong?" Mardi flew to him, panic seizing her. Had he choked? Had a heart attack?

He wasn't moving, didn't appear to be even breathing. She acted instinctively, lifting his frail body and lowering

him to the floor. She checked his airways and started CPR.
Between breathing into his mouth and pumping his chest,
she screamed for Nicky, who was getting ready for school.
"Nicky, come quickly! Hurry!" For once he obeyed her
instantly.

"Nicky, grab the phone and dial triple O—that's OOO.
Tell them to send an ambulance quickly." She continued
CPR. "Tell them your grandpa's not breathing. And give
them our address. Then run and fetch Cain and Ben."

Everything happened in a blur after that. Cain and Ben
turning up, the ambulance arriving within minutes, the paramedics working on Grandpa. But Mardi knew in her heart
that their efforts were futile.

She watched numbly, too shocked to react. How could
this happen? Everything had been going so well. Despite
his age, Grandpa had recovered amazingly well from his
hip operation.

She felt Cain's arms around her and swayed back against
him. "Please don't give up," she begged the paramedics.

"He's gone, Mrs. Sinclair. I'm sorry." They rose to their
feet. "Has your grandfather had any heart problems? Been
short of breath? Complained of feeling ill?"

She shook her head. "He had a hip operation earlier this
month." She felt numb. "But he was making good progress."

"I suggest you call his doctor. He'll know what to do."

"I'll call him," Cain offered as the paramedics left.
"Just give me his number, Mardi."

The next few days passed in a fog. The day of their
wedding came and went, the registry office ceremony post-
poned until after Grandpa's funeral. Mardi hardly noticed,
hardly cared. She was still in shock. The doctor had put
his death down to a massive blood clot.

Cain did all he could for her, arranging the funeral, notifying Ernie's few remaining friends, keeping the two boys occupied, generally showing he was there for her. She seemed grateful, but was disturbingly remote. Nothing he said to her seemed to get through.

The distress in her lovely hazel eyes shook Cain as few things ever had. In the past he'd been able to detach himself from other people's pain, but Mardi's silent agony seemed to weave into his very soul.

A few days after the funeral he came home to find her in tears at last, weeping uncontrollably.

"You don't have to handle this alone, Mardi,' he said, gathering her in his arms. Pushing her damp hair back from her face he began to stroke her soft cheek, feeling her wet tears under his fingers.

"Oh, Cain, I miss him so," she choked out between sobs. His chest felt so warm and comforting, his compassion releasing the last of her pent-up grief. "I loved him so much. I owe Grandpa everything!"

She seemed to realize what she'd said, and who she'd said it to, and became flustered. "I—I don't mean money or material things. He—he never had a lot of money. Other things were more important to him—values, ideals, caring, a stable upbringing. He loved me and m-made a lot of sacrifices…" Her voice trailed off, her breath quivering in the wake of her tears.

Cain buried his lips in her silky-smooth hair. *Sacrifices…love…* He wondered when *he'd* ever made sacrifices for anybody, or if he even knew the meaning of the word *love*.

Truly, this woman and her grandfather were a revelation…this family who valued people and the basic virtues above money and possessions. It made him realize more than ever what a coldhearted, ruthless existence he'd been leading all these years. Money, power and position had been his goals and he'd shut out every human emotion to achieve them. And yet none of those things had satisfied him in the end, leaving him with an empty, bitter taste and a lead weight in his gut.

Maybe Mardi would be his salvation.

He tilted her chin and kissed her swollen eyelids. She uttered a soft sound and he kissed them again, with more passion. Then suddenly he was kissing her face, her cheeks, her throat. She was clinging to him as if his kisses had unleashed something inside her, too.

Mardi responded without thought, the pressure of his lips igniting fires she'd kept firmly under control for the past month. She opened her mouth under the sensuous urging of his, wanting oblivion, wanting mind-numbing sensations, anything to blot out the despair she'd been feeling for the past few days. This was no time to think, only to feel…to forget…

And Cain, in the grip of the same avalanche of released tension, was prepared to do anything she wanted. He moved his hands over her body, sliding them underneath her shirt, feeling the silky smoothness of her skin beneath his fingers.

His lips found hers again, opening in a long, desperate kiss that sent spirals of heat through him, flames he felt scorching through her body, too.

With their mouths still locked, he lifted her in his arms and carried her into the bedroom, where they tumbled, limbs entangled, onto the bed. Luckily, there were no small boys in the house to hear them.

With gasping breaths and sweat-dampened bodies, they writhed and strained against each other, neither wanting to stop, or even thinking about stopping, both too swept up in the swirling fire that engulfed them.

Mardi couldn't remember ever feeling such exquisite, mindless passion. She almost gasped out the words "I love you,'' but forced herself back to reality just in time. Love and emotion weren't meant to be part of this marriage. The cold realization hit her before she could lose control completely. She rolled away from him, moaning, ''I'd rather wait until we're married!''

''If that's what you want, Mardi.'' Cain's thickened voice drifted back to her. ''You see, our marriage is going to be good for both of us.''

He still hadn't spoken of love, or feelings, and he didn't want to hear it from her, because love, emotional involvement, wasn't part of their bargain. She wondered, for a fleeting moment, if Cain Templar had ever felt love, even for Sylvia.

Maybe their marriage *would* work, if she didn't expect too much. And she didn't…. She wouldn't—ever again.

Two days later they were married at the local registry office, with the two little boys excitedly looking on and a neighbor of Cain's, Dr. Graham Bartlett, Ben's family doctor, and Graham's psychiatrist wife, Kate, as witnesses.

None of Cain's business colleagues, or any friends, were there. ''Once you're settled in,'' he'd promised her, ''we'll arrange a get-together with a few friends, so they can meet you as my wife.''

His *wife*. Mardi shuddered to think what Tiffany's reaction would be. Maybe Cain had already told her. Maybe she was already out of their lives. *But as Cain's business partner, how could she be?*

Mardi was wearing a lightweight summer suit and she'd made a posy of yellow roses from Cain's garden. A yellow satin ribbon tied back swathes of her hair, the rest falling loose.

Cain wore a gray business suit with a oyster-gray shirt and a yellow tie to match her flowers, a thoughtful gesture that touched her, perhaps more than it should. He'd even told her she looked lovely, which she appreciated, too, even knowing it was a lie. But just hearing the compliment was uplifting.

The simple ceremony was over quickly. When the celebrant announced them husband and wife and said, "You may kiss the bride," Cain bent his head and kissed her. Mardi felt the same instant response she always did, brief and public as it was. She felt a little dizzy when he drew back. She turned quickly to smile at the boys, avoiding Cain's eyes, afraid of what her own might reveal. What *did* she feel? she wondered. A yearning for something more?

She was now Mardi Templar. And soon Nicky would be a Templar, too, a true brother to Ben, when the adoption procedure Cain had already put into motion was finalized.

The Bartletts left them after the ceremony to go back to their busy medical practices, and Cain took his new wife and family to a child-friendly restaurant for lunch—not a place, Mardi reflected, where he'd be likely to bump into any of his high-flying colleagues.

They spent the afternoon moving into Cain's big house. There wasn't much to move, so it didn't take too long.

Cain offered Nicky the room opposite Ben's, but Ben insisted on his new brother sharing his own big bedroom, which already had a spare bed.

"We'll give it a try," Cain agreed, "but if you boys play up or don't go to sleep at night, Nicky goes to his own room, okay?"

"Okay," the boys chorused, then dissolved into giggles. They were ecstatic about being true brothers at last, and Ben seemed genuinely excited at having Mardi for a mother. When he asked her if he could call her "Mummy," she felt tears stinging her eyelids.

She glanced at Cain, wondering how he would take the idea.

He smiled, with a warmth in his eyes that she wasn't sure was for her or for Ben. If only, she thought. "You may call Mardi Mummy, Ben," Cain said, "if Nicky will call me Dad. Or Daddy."

There was a short, awkward silence. Nicky had only ever called him Mr. Templar and was still a little in awe of him. But not so much that he couldn't find the courage to speak up, even if the words that came out were barely more than a squeak. "But you're not my daddy. My daddy's dead."

Mardi's throat tightened. She'd been so sure Nicky was happy about the new arrangement. He hadn't mentioned Darrell for weeks. She slipped an arm round her son's thin shoulders and felt his tension. "It doesn't mean you have to forget your daddy, Nicky. You can still have his picture in your room, and you can still love him and talk about him. But Daddy's gone now, and you have a new daddy, just as Ben has a new mummy. If you'd rather call him Cain…"

Ben gave a snort, showing what he thought of that idea. "Call him Dad, like I do," he advised Nicky. "Not Daddy—Daddy's only for babies."

Nicky nodded shyly, and Mardi, relieved, said to Ben with a smile, "Does that mean you'd rather call me Mum than Mummy?"

Ben's lips stretched in a grin. "Nicky calls you Mummy, so I will, too," he said, and the matter was settled.

The only one missing from the move to the big house was Grandpa. Mardi wondered, with a pang, what Ernie would have thought of the move. She smiled mistily, imagining him grumbling, "It doesn't feel right, moving into *that Jezebel's* house."

And it didn't. Sylvia's influence was everywhere in the

palatial house. The only thing missing, surprisingly, was a
photograph of her, or a portrait.

Had Cain been so hurt by his wife's affair that he
couldn't bear to see his wife's smiling face following him
around the house, imagining she was taunting him? His *first*
wife, she corrected herself. *She* was his wife now.

Would Cain want any photographs of his *new* wife in
his house? Well, too bad if he didn't, Mardi decided. She
intended to display photographs of herself and Nicky along-
side the photographs she'd seen of Ben.

Mardi chewed on her lip. Now that she was Cain's wife,
maybe she should try to draw the boy out. Naturally she
would talk to Cain first, pointing out that it wasn't healthy
for Ben never to mention his mother. But this was hardly
the time.

She took a deep breath as Cain led her into the spacious
master bedroom. Like the pristine white rooms downstairs,
this room also had Sylvia's stamp, with its rich brocaded
drapes and matching bedspread, its thick-piled ice-blue carpet and Louis XVI-style dressing table and chairs. Was
Sylvia's presence going to haunt their lives forever?

Mardi's gaze was drawn back to the bed. A giant king-
size bed with a luxurious draped silk bedhead and piles of
exotic cushions in bright colors, looking as opulent as
something from the *Arabian Nights.*

Panic seized her. *How could she sleep there, in the very
bed he'd shared with Sylvia?*

Cain caught her look. ''How about we ditch the bedspread and cushions and that draped stuff above the bed,
and buy a doona?'' His voice was soft, calming. ''Go out
tomorrow and choose one, Mardi. I know this isn't your
style or taste.''

Not your style or taste... No, Mardi thought with a grimace, I'm not the glamorous, opulent, sophisticated type.

I'm the ordinary, homemaking, motherly type. The comfortable, homespun, doona type.

The marriage-of-convenience type.

"It's not my style, either," Cain drawled, "but I haven't had the time or made the effort, I guess, to do anything about it. I'm not much good at decorating."

The admission that he didn't care for the style, either, surprised her.

"Besides, I'd like you to make our home more livable," Cain said. "We're going to have two lively boys racing around with dirty hands and muddy shoes...."

She tilted her head at him. "You'd allow grubby little boys to race around your beautiful house?"

Cain winced. He never would have tolerated it while Sylvia was around, he thought. Sylvia wouldn't have a thing out of place, wouldn't allow a dirty mark to mar her perfect house. But Mardi wasn't Sylvia and circumstances had changed. Even a man could change.

"Did you think I was going to keep them confined to their bedroom? Or shoved down into the basement?" His mouth curved in a wry grin. "The gym, by the way, can be converted quite easily into a kids' rumpus room. They'll need a room like that as they grow older."

As they grow older... Mardi swallowed. She hadn't looked that far into the future.

She felt a sobering jolt of reality. She was Cain Templar's wife. She would be living with him for as long as their sons needed both of them...maybe even longer, if it worked out. Tonight, as his wife, she would be sharing his bed...*this* bed.

Cain saw her gaze flick back to the bed and felt like kicking himself. Damn, he should have realized! It wasn't the extravagant décor that was troubling her as much as the thought of sleeping in the bed she imagined he'd shared

with Sylvia. Only, Sylvia *hadn't* slept here…at least, no
since Ben was a baby.

"For the record, Sylvia slept in the guest room next door
not in here." He kept his voice devoid of expression. "She
said I disturbed her beauty sleep. She redecorated the room
so that only a woman would want to spend time in it."

"You didn't *sleep* together?" Mardi's eyes widened
What kind of marriage had it been? "Is that why your wife
had an affair with my husband?" The question leapt out.

A sardonic half smile tugged at Cain's lips. "My wife
was having affairs long before she met your husband." He
sounded resigned rather than bitter.

So the affair hadn't been Sylvia's first. Well, no wonder,
Mardi thought with a tinge of irony, if they never slept
together. "And I suppose you were, too?" she challenged,
only to add in the same breath, "Sorry, Cain. What you
did in the past is none of my business." She didn't want
to know.

"Sleeping in separate rooms didn't mean we never had
sex." There was a weary cynicism in his voice. "She was
still my wife. I was still her husband. She just disliked
sharing a bed."

Mardi glanced up at him. Had *sex,* he'd said. Not *made
love.* What a cold-blooded marriage it must have been. She
drew in a tremulous breath, remembering their passionate
kisses the other day. At least their sex life would sizzle,
even if he didn't love her. But would *she* be able to separate
sex from feeling, from emotion? She already felt far too
much.

"Did you love your wife?" she asked, curiosity overrid-
ing her reluctance to delve into his past.

"Love?" His eyes grew remote again, impossible to
read. "I don't think I've ever known what love is. We both

vanted the same things. We were both equally ambitious, qually driven.''

Mardi sat silently. It was the most revealing he'd been o far. She decided that the time had come to grab the bull >y the horns and broach the subject that had been nagging at her. "I notice there are no photographs of Sylvia in the 10use.'' She gulped, and pressed on. "Even Ben has no >hotographs of his mother. Do you think that's fair, Cain, o your son?''

There was a long, crackling pause. When he finally did 'espond, his voice was toneless, his face carved in stone, howing no emotion at all.

"I wasn't the one who removed Sylvia's photographs, Mardi. I came home from work one night and found that Ben had torn every photo from its frame and ripped them all to shreds."

Mardi was appalled. "Why would Ben do a thing like that?''

"I guess he was mad at his mother for leaving him. Some of the kids from kindergarten taunted him after the accident for having a mother who'd run off with another man. Ben thought she hadn't cared about him, and I'm not sure that she really did. Not that I've ever said as much to Ben, naturally.''

"Oh, Cain, poor Ben." Had Nicky been taunted, too, about his father, and never said anything? Her heart wrenched at the thought.

"He seems to be over it now…thanks to you and Nicky. And having me home a bit more is helping." Cain's soft voice had a soothing effect. "I have other photographs of his mother that I'd put away in a cupboard. I can give him those if he ever changes his mind. Seeing Nicky with pho- tos of his father might do the trick. Or maybe not. He looks on *you* as his mother now.''

Mardi blinked, and swallowed. "And I look on Ben a son," she whispered.

"Well, now…" Cain changed the subject. "Why don you get yourself settled in while I make some phone call The first one will be to a local catering service. I don want you cooking on our wedding day."

Our wedding day. And tonight was their wedding nigh Her first night as Cain's wife. She felt a surge of longin of delicious, remembered sensation, and realized she coul hardly wait.

Chapter Twelve

Living in Cain's grand house as his wife was vastly different from living in his granny flat as his cook and baby-sitter. Mardi found she had little to do during school hours, because Elena and Joe still came in every day to do the housework and tend to the garden.

It was a pampered existence, and Mardi, not used to having things done for her, felt useless and ill at ease in her new role.

She'd never been one for shopping sprees or bridge parties or lunches, and anyway, most of her former friends had drifted out of her life. Cooking, knitting and sewing had filled her spare time and had helped her to save money. And last year she'd had her part-time job at the girls' school.

But there was little to do here. Determined to make herself useful, she concentrated on making subtle changes to the house—moving fragile ornaments to safer spots and replacing them with framed photographs, favorite books and more practical ornaments, buying scatter rugs to throw over the white carpet in the so-called "family room," and throwing fringed ponchos over the white armchairs and sofas.

She didn't touch the formal sitting room or dining room and she'd declared them off-limits to the boys.

Although Cain had given her a free hand with his checkbook, she couldn't bring herself to spend his money on brand-new furnishings, or even on re-covering the existing furniture in more practical fabrics. The expensive drapes and the pure white carpets would also have to be changed even though they were still as good as new, and even the delicate lamps and exquisite side tables would be wrong and have to go. It would be a terrible waste, and the potential cost made her shudder.

And besides, Cain hadn't exactly encouraged any radical or permanent changes to his house. He'd commended her minor efforts to make it more livable, but he'd said cryptically, "We might leave any major redecorating for the time being.... I've some ideas, but they can wait for now. There's no rush." Maybe he didn't trust her ideas, or want her changing his house. *Sylvia's* house.

Mardi wondered if she would ever feel comfortable or at home in this vast, elegant, pristine white mansion. The whole place was wrong for a growing, rough-and-tumble family, and it was wrong for *her*.

She didn't see much of Cain in those first couple of weeks. He was working longer hours again—to catch up on time lost, she presumed—and he'd even had the odd night or two away on business. She missed him dreadfully on those nights, and huddled between pillows so that she wouldn't feel so alone in the big king-size bed. She'd come to yearn for the nights spent in his arms, and was amazed each time at how quickly they both became aroused, and how blissfully exciting it was every time.

Near the end of the second week Cain said, "We've been invited to a birthday celebration on Saturday night. Gerald, one of my partners, is turning forty and throwing a big bash at his house. It'll be an opportunity to let them all know we're married. I know you'd prefer to do it this way—quietly, without any fuss or big announcements."

"They'll think you've lost your mind, marrying me," she said, voicing her qualms aloud. "And they'll think I'm a scheming little gold digger who's got to you through your son."

Cain's face clouded and for a second he looked positively dangerous, his hands seizing her arms in a fierce grip. "They'll think nothing of the sort. They've seen the sort of woman you are and often ask after you—they know you've been through a lot lately. They like you, Mardi. Who couldn't like you?"

Was he saying *he* liked her? *Like,* she thought pensively. Would liking and good sex be enough for a lifetime of marriage?

"Go out and buy a new dress tomorrow," Cain said. "It's a black-tie affair—they love an excuse to dress up, even for a party at home. No. Better still, I'll take you to Double Bay myself and we'll choose something together."

Was he afraid she'd choose the wrong thing and shame him? Or spend too much? *Double Bay,* he'd said...home of the most exclusive boutiques in Sydney. Well, he couldn't be worried about the price if he was taking her there.

They hired a baby-sitter, a university student recommended by someone at Cain's office, to look after the two boys for the evening. When Bryony arrived, Mardi was already dressed and ready to go. She said good-night to the boys, who were already in their pajamas playing games on Ben's computer, and headed downstairs to join Cain.

"You look beautiful," he said, and she glowed like a teenager, even though she wasn't sure if he was referring to her or the dress he'd bought her.

It was very simple—a sleek ankle-length shift with spaghetti straps—but the bronze fabric and the expert cut made it special. For a change she was wearing her hair loose. She'd washed it and blown it dry until it shone, and she knew that under lights it gleamed with golden-bronze highlights, picked up from her dress.

She wore only drop-shaped amber earrings. Cain had wanted to buy her an exquisite diamond necklace and earrings or an equally exquisite gold necklace with matching earrings, but she'd held out for the amber earrings alone. She hadn't wanted to waltz into Gerald's home looking as if she'd married Cain for the glittering jewelry he could lavish on her.

Still, it was an ordeal walking into Gerald's imposing home, a majestic Edwardian mansion with high decorative ceilings, richly adorned walls and beautiful antique furniture. Several other couples were already there, and a hush fell as she and Cain stepped into the huge reception area.

Gerald and his wife, Ellen, hurried over to greet them.

"Cain! And..." Their eyes swiveled to Mardi, who wished the floor would open up and swallow her.

"You know Mardi, don't you?" Cain said smoothly, holding her arm securely in his. "I'm happy to say that Mardi is now my wife."

As their hosts greeted this revelation with stunned looks and exclamations of polite surprise, Cain swept on. "And Ben has a new brother...Mardi's son Nicky, Ben's best friend. You met Nicky on the boat. Gerald, happy birthday, old man.'' He thrust out his hand and the focus of attention, mercifully, moved away from Mardi.

Another couple arrived, and Cain grabbed her arm and led her deeper into the room. Other couples clustered round them, smiling and congratulating them. The nearest guests had overheard Cain's announcement and the word had spread like wildfire. Mardi wondered how sincere their felicitations were. The men's smiles seemed genuine enough, but she wasn't so sure about the women, her feminine intuition picking up wary vibes behind their bright smiles as they looked her over.

There was no sign of Tiffany. She either hadn't arrived yet or wasn't coming. Mardi prayed for the latter.

''Do you play bridge?'' one of the wives asked her, drawing her into a huddle of women as Cain was swallowed up elsewhere.

''I'm afraid not.''

''You could always have lessons.'' A faint sniff accompanied the suggestion.

''You'll have to come to one of our fashion parades,'' another woman piped up. ''It's always a very social occasion, with lunch thrown in. All in aid of charity, of course.''

''Do you play tennis?'' someone else asked. ''Some of us play at a private home every Tuesday. Purely social, with a lot of giggling and gossip. Maybe you'd like to come along one day?''

Mardi knew they were testing her out, to see whether she was going to ''fit in.'' Inside, her heart was sinking. Was this going to be her life from now on?

''Of course, you and Cain have your *own* tennis court, haven't you?'' one of the wives said with an ingenuous smile. ''We all know *he* seldom uses it—he's always too busy—and Sylvia didn't play at all. Such a waste of a perfectly good tennis court. But if *you* play...''

It was a hint, if ever there was one. "Well, I haven't played for some time," Mardi admitted, not mentioning that she'd dragged Cain onto the court only last weekend for some hits, and had quite enjoyed it.

"But you're welcome to use our court during the week," she offered. Spending one day a week playing tennis wouldn't be so bad. It was the idle gossip that bothered her.

"Oh my, here's Tiffany," gushed one of the women. "Making the grand entrance as usual."

Relieved as she felt at no longer being the center of attention, Mardi's spirits dipped as her gaze swung round. Tiffany had paused just inside the room, secure in the knowledge that all eyes would be on her—which they were, of course—and openly savoring the limelight.

She looked stunning in a vibrant red, slinky little number that clung to every curve. Her tumble of black hair gleamed like polished ebony, highlighting her glossy red lips and flashing dark eyes. She was waving a hand about, perhaps to show off the glittering bracelet on her wrist. Diamonds, obviously. *Real* diamonds.

Mardi wondered if this was how Cain had wanted *her* to look. Glittery and glamorous, the focus of all eyes.

She turned away so abruptly that she spilled the contents of her glass down the front of her new dress. She looked down in dismay to see a wet champagne stain darkening the bronze bodice.

"Excuse me," she whispered, and slipped away, grabbing the nearest waitress, who gave her a bottle of soda water and directed her upstairs to a luxurious en suite bathroom off the main bedroom.

She looked in the mirror and winced. Oh, great. Elegant and sophisticated one minute, an embarrassing mess the next. What a clumsy dolt she was. She picked up a hand towel, poured soda water onto it and dabbed at the stain.

"I suppose we can just leave our things here on the bed." A woman's voice wafted in from the bedroom. "We won't need our stoles, unless we go out on the terrace later."

Another voice spoke up, in a conspiratorial tone. "Well, what do you think of Cain Templar marrying again? What a shock! You know who she is, of course? The widow of Sylvia's lover!"

Mardi froze. They were talking about *her*.

"I suppose that's what brought them together. The tragedy. The shared humiliation. The urge to cry on each other's shoulders."

The other woman chuckled. "Can you imagine Cain Templar crying on anyone's shoulder? Nah... Frank says it was their sons who brought them together. They're best friends. They both go to St. Mark's."

"Who is she, anyway? Where does she come from? What's her background? She couldn't be more different from Sylvia, could she? She has none of Sylvia's glamour and pizzazz. And she's obviously not much of a party-goer—I've never seen her anywhere. She doesn't even play bridge, Diane told me."

"Well, it's plain he's only married her to give his son a mother. Why else would he choose someone like her? He could have had any woman he wanted," the woman added with a smirk in her voice. "At least his new wife doesn't look the type to play around.... She looks *safe*."

Safe... Mardi's mouth dipped. Yeah, you're spot on, babe. He married me because he knew he'd feel *safe* with me. He wouldn't be tempted to fall in love with me. Her mouth dipped farther. Love? Cain Templar didn't even know what love was. He'd told her as much.

"It's a wonder he didn't marry Tiffany," the other woman mused aloud. "She's been after him long enough."

Mardi's senses prickled. Was it common knowledge that the two had had an affair?

"Can you imagine Tiffany bringing up a child? Not that having a kid ever cramped Sylvia's style. She often used to say, what are nannies and baby-sitters *for?*"

Mardi felt a choking sensation in her throat. She couldn't listen to any more of this! But how could she march out and confront them? How could she maintain her dignity, looking like this? She glared into the mirror at the dark patch on her dress. She would have to dry off a bit before she let anyone see her, or they'd have even more to snigger about.

"We'd better go. I'm dying for a drink." The voices, mercifully, faded at last.

Mardi slumped over the vanity. When she looked up again she caught sight of a hair dryer attached to the wall. It wouldn't matter if she made a noise now. She switched it on and directed the heat onto the front of her dress. The damp stain was beginning to fade already.

As she stood drying herself, the words she'd overheard boiled and seethed through her mind.

"Mardi," she growled to herself, "you've let other people and their needs rule your life for too long. You've lost your identity as a woman, as a *person*. It's time you took control of your life."

She felt a zing of excitement. She'd always wanted some time to herself, time to do her own thing. Well, now she *had* the time. Her newly pampered existence gave her the chance of a lifetime, the opportunity she'd been looking for all her life and had only now realized was here at last.

She knew exactly what she was going to do. Something she'd dreamed of doing since she'd scribbled stories and

poems as a child, and made up stories in her head to tell
Nicky at bedtime. She was going to write a book. A novel.
A romantic novel.

She could do it. Romantic novels had been an easy read
and an escape. She'd needed escape. She'd become hooked
on romances, and had long dreamed of writing one herself,
only, she hadn't had the time or the opportunity until now.

Now she had all the time in the world.

She found herself grinning at her reflection in the mirror.
Tomorrow… She would start tomorrow.

The mark on her dress, she saw in relief, had vanished,
no permanent stain remaining. Whew!

With new confidence and a heady sense of exhilaration
at what lay ahead, she left the bathroom, crossed the bedroom and headed for the stairs. Only to meet Tiffany on
the landing.

Tiffany's beautiful face had contorted into a look of pure
evil, venting such fury and malice that Mardi thought the
wicked witch of her childhood fairy tales and nightmares
had come to life. She felt chilled to the bone.

"I knew you were determined to sink your claws into
him." Tiffany spat the words at her. "I knew you'd use
his son to worm your way into his life. Well, if you think
you're going to win his heart as well as his money and his
name, you can forget it. His heart belongs to *me*. He's told
me so, and shown it many a time. And he's *proved* it—
with this!" She waved her wrist under Mardi's nose, a triumphant gleam in her eye.

The diamond bracelet, sparkling under the overhead
chandelier, drew Mardi's eyes like a magnet. *Cain* had
given it to her?

Somehow Mardi found her voice, hoarse as it was.
"What Cain did before we were married is of no concern
to me."

Tiffany gave a harsh, mocking laugh. "He gave it to me last Tuesday night when he took me out to dinner. I understand you've been married for a couple of weeks. And mighty quiet he's kept it—even from me."

Mardi felt the floor tilt. Last *Tuesday?* Cain *had* gone out to dinner last Tuesday, she recalled. He'd told her he was meeting some businessmen from New York. He hadn't mentioned Tiffany.

Mardi felt as if she were tumbling into the same black pit of despair she'd fallen into when Grandpa died. She'd thought Tiffany was out of their lives.

The rat. No wonder he'd been working long hours and having nights away. He'd been seeing *her.* He wanted to have his cake and eat it, too. As long as he kept the little wife happy at home, and his son well cared for, he felt he could do as he wished.

Oh, Mardi, you poor fool. You knew what the deal was. *No emotional involvement.* But it was too late. She *was* emotionally involved. She found herself grasping at straws. "Some men give generous gifts when they break off a relationship with a woman." She forced the words out.

Tiffany's taunting laugh cut through her like a hacksaw. "Believe that, darling, if it makes you feel better. But I've yet to meet a man who'll spend around a hundred thousand dollars on a woman he never wants to see again."

A hundred *thousand?* It couldn't be true. "If he *did* give it to you," she croaked.

"Oh, he gave it to me, all right. Why don't you ask him? Just be warned, he won't deny it." The scarlet lips curved. "In our world a wise woman would turn a blind eye."

In our world. The flashy, high-flying world Cain belonged to. The world her late husband had coveted and she'd always despised.

She tossed back her head in a gesture of defiance. She'd

agreed to this marriage for her family's sake...for Ben's sake...and for them she'd do it all again. And heaven help her, deep down she'd wanted it for herself, too. The first time she'd ever set eyes on Cain Templar, even before she knew who he was, she'd fallen under his potent spell and she'd been bewitched ever since. She deserved everything that fate threw at her.

Only, she wasn't going to wallow about at the mercy of the Fates anymore. *You're taking control of your life, remember?* Tomorrow she was going to start a brand-new career, one that she would be in full control of and that she alone would be responsible for. And heaven help anyone who tried to stop her.

"I must rejoin my husband," she said pointedly, summoning her flagging dignity. At least Tiffany couldn't dispute the fact the Cain was her husband. He'd chosen to marry *her*.

Cain was getting worried. One of the wives had told him that Mardi had spilled something down her dress and had gone to deal with it. But that was ages ago. Where the hell *was* she?

As he pushed his way through the crush, a gong sounded, deep and resonant, announcing that dinner was served. How Gerald loved his old-time gong, a relic of the past, handed down by his grandfather. Spying Mardi, he made a beeline for her.

"Ah, there you are. Are you okay?"

"Never better," Mardi said brightly. Too brightly, he thought. "Sorry I took so long, but I spilled some champagne on my dress. Luckily I don't seem to have ruined it. While I was waiting for it to dry, I came to a decision." Her eyes met his, clear and steady and determined.

"A decision...about what?" What momentous decision

had she come up with? Would it complicate things, jus
when—

"I have some time on my hands, now that the boys ar
at school and my life has settled down a bit—"

"You want to go back to work? Or back to university?"
Now that, he thought, might be awkward.

"I want to write a book. A romantic novel." Her eye.
challenged him, defying him to put a damper on the idea
"It's something I've always wanted to do. I thought I coul
use Ben's computer while the boys are at school."

Cain felt a flicker of relief. "That's a wonderful idea
I'll buy you a laptop. And your own printer. You won'
want to be confined to Ben's room. With a laptop, you car
work anywhere."

The gong sounded again, more urgently this time. "We'c
better move into the dining room or Ellen will get in ⟨
flurry." He cupped her elbow and steered her away, following the crowd. "You can tell me about it over dinner."

But there was no chance. The dinner was buffet-style
with a delectable feast spread out on the table for everyone
to help themselves. With so many people milling about.
filling their plates and looking for chairs, they became sep-
arated in the melee. Mardi ended up sitting wedged between a couple of women guests, while he was left standing
in a corner with some male colleagues. But he kept her
under his eye.

At least Tiffany was keeping away from both of them,
he thought, glancing around. She had a huddle of panting
males clustered round her, ogling her and hanging on to
her every word. When Tiffany failed to be the center of
attention, Cain mused dryly, she would curl up and die.

As his gaze swerved from Tiffany back to Mardi, he
caught his wife's eye. Damn! She'd seen him watching
Tiffany and thought he'd been ogling her like all the others!

He tried to reassure Mardi by smiling and sending a special message with his eyes, but she'd already turned away. Friendly and polite as she was being, he could tell she didn't feel comfortable with these people, or with their idle small talk. Parties and society bashes might have been Sylvia's idea of a good time, but they plainly weren't Mardi's. And he was relieved to know it.

Tonight he would tell her. He'd wanted to wait until he was sure it was the right thing for all of them and that he had it all worked out. Now the necessary time had passed and he was sure. He was ready to make the commitment.

He just hoped Mardi would feel the same way.

Chapter Thirteen

As the party swung on, Mardi's head began to ache. It wasn't just the noise and the champagne she'd consumed, it was the tension of being in the same house as Tiffany.

After dinner there were a few witty speeches, and then the entertainment began. Gerald and Ellen had engaged a professional female singer who sang like an angel, a brilliant male comedian whose jokes were genuinely funny and a magician who amazed everyone with his tricks.

Mardi was relieved that she didn't have to make conversation while they were being entertained. She'd pulled her chair into a corner, next to a potted palm, in the hope that it would shield her from Tiffany's malignant leers.

Cain was standing at the back of the room with other male guests. She avoided looking his way, though her mind kept conjuring unsettling images of him gazing into Tiffany's eyes across an intimate table for two, and tenderly placing diamonds round his colleague's slender wrist.

When the performance was over, a bearded young man with a guitar joined the pianist and struck up with some

feet-stomping dance music. Those who didn't wish to dance
spilled into other rooms or out onto the terrace to gather in
groups and indulge in more champagne.

Mardi seized her chance to grab Cain. "Do you think
we could slip off now?" she asked under cover of the music. "I don't want to keep Bryony up too late. I mean, it
already *is* late…."

"You wouldn't like to have a dance first?" Shimmering
blue eyes held her gaze captive. "It would give me an
excuse to hold you."

Her body heated in instant response, even as her mind
rejected the temptation. She didn't want to be held by Cain.
Not tonight. Not with Tiffany in the same house, flaunting
the expensive bauble he'd given her.

"Would you mind if we didn't?" She severed eye contact, letting her eyelashes flicker away. "I have a bit of a
headache."

"Oh, in that case we'll leave right now. We'll say good-
night to Gerald and Ellen and slip away quietly."

"Without saying good-night to…your other friends?"
she couldn't resist asking.

"They won't even notice. If they do, we'll just say we
have to go. They know we have young children."

They know we have young children. Mardi's eyes felt
prickly as they went in search of their hosts. Cain thought
of them as a family now…. She and Nicky, he and Ben.
He cared about his family—he'd shown it many times in
these past weeks. He was doing his best to make them all
happy, to make his new *wife* happy—even in bed.

She pressed her knuckles to her temple—and covered up
quickly, pushing back a stray lock of hair as they met up
with Gerald and Ellen. Minutes later she was sitting in
Cain's luxury car, heading for home. She leaned back and
shut her eyes, making it clear she didn't want to talk.

How was she going to go on? How was she going to
pretend she didn't know, and worse, didn't care? Bringing
his affair out into the open would only make things worse.
She knew that from experience...that a man in lust wasn'
going to give up the woman he desired just because his
wife wasn't happy about it.

By the time they arrived home, the throbbing pain in her
head had become a thunderous torment. *What was she going to do?*

The house was peacefully silent when they walked in.
Bryony was curled up on the elegant white sofa in the elegant white family room, reading a book. She jumped up,
assuring them that the boys had been good and had gone
to sleep without any trouble, though she admitted it might
have been a bit later than their usual time.

While Cain was paying Bryony and seeing her to her
car, Mardi slipped upstairs to the boys' room. Seeing their
sleeping angelic faces brought a well of tears to her eyes.
How could she jeopardize their lives, their future happiness,
by having a confrontation with Cain and risking what they
had now?

She couldn't! The boys had been through too much already.

Suddenly Mardi felt Cain's arm slip round her shoulders
and a tremor shook through her. She hadn't heard him coming. She steeled herself not to feel anything, hoping he
would put her reaction down to surprise at his silent approach, not to a shudder of anguish at his touch.

"They look so innocent and vulnerable when they're
asleep, don't they?" he murmured.

"They're beautiful," she said huskily. "I love them
both." She forced out the *love* word to show him that although there was to be no love between their parents, no
love at least on his side, she could still express her love for

her boys. Maybe, one day, in the dim future of their "practical" marriage, when his affair with Tiffany had burned out, her coldhearted husband would come to learn what love was.

She trembled. He wasn't so coldhearted when they made love in the big king-size bed, when their souls seemed to converge and soar as one, and scorching passion rocketed them to heart-rending heights.

"I must get to bed," she choked out, slipping from his grasp. She tore off her new dress and snatched up a pair of shapeless pajamas, diving into the ensuite bathroom before Cain could join her in the bedroom. When she came out, Cain was undressing. He'd already peeled off his dinner jacket and dress shirt and was in the process of discarding his black trousers. Averting her eyes, she slipped into her side of the big bed and turned her back on him.

"I think it's great that you're going to write a book," Cain commented, sounding sincere.

She frowned into her pillow, wondering if he was pleased because it would keep her happy and occupied. A busy, fulfilled wife was less likely to ask probing questions about the nights he spent elsewhere. "Well, I'm going to try," she mumbled.

The bed creaked as his weight came down behind her. Close behind. She could feel his warmth through the thick cotton pajamas. She groaned aloud.

"Are you all right?" Cain asked, sliding an arm round her.

"I'm very tired." Her voice was a husky croak. "And my headache's killing me."

"I know just the cure for that." His hand slipped under her pajama top and cupped her breast. As she tensed, her nipples hardening against her will, his heated body pressed into her from behind, showing that he was already aroused.

But had *she* aroused him? Or was he imagining she was Tiffany?

"I feel sick!" It was a strangled gasp. "I need some air!" She wriggled out of his grasp and rolled off the big bed. She couldn't make love to him tonight. She needed to get away from him. She needed some fresh air.

She started running. But instead of heading for the glass doors leading out onto the upstairs balcony, she made for the bedroom door and scuttled along the passage to the stairs.

Stinging tears blinded her. She missed the top stair and cried out as she tumbled headlong down the flight of stairs.

"Oh, my God! *Mardi!*" A pain such as Cain had never known before pierced him like a slashing sword as he reached the top of the stairs. She couldn't be dead...oh, dear God, *no!*

He hurtled down the stairs three, four at a time, unaware of what he was doing, aware only of the still body lying at the foot of the stairs. The woman he loved...

Why had he never told her he loved her? A frantic cry tore from his throat. "Oh God, Mardi, please by okay!"

He rolled her gently over, leaning closer to listen for a breath, a ray of hope. She was so still...so pale... His gut wrenched in fear. "Mardi, my precious, you have to be all right. I love you. I love you more than my life!" And then he felt the warmth of her breath on his face. "Thank God! You're still alive."

She moaned, her eyes flickering open. What was Cain saying? And was that a *tear* in his eye?

"Oh, Mardi, my dearest, you'll be all right, darling, don't move. I'll call an ambulance. You might have broken something. And you could have a concussion." It was her spine

Cain was worried about most of all. "Just lie still while I make that call."

She reached out a shaky hand. "No. No ambulance. I—I think I'm just sore and bruised. Just give me a minute. Every bone in my body is hurting, but I don't think I've broken anything."

"Let's just make sure. If you won't let me call an ambulance, I'll call Graham. Don't try to get up!" He left her just long enough to call his doctor friend.

As they waited for him to arrive, Cain cradled her in his arms, repeating over and over again how much he loved her. Now that he'd unlocked the words, unlocked his heart, he couldn't seem to hold them back. Almost losing her had ripped the icy chains from his heart and soul and exposed them like a raw, gaping wound.

"I love you, Mardi, and I always will," he murmured, his lips in her hair.

She turned her face away. "How can you love me when you're still seeing Tiffany?"

"I *work* with Tiffany," he corrected her gently. "I'm not *seeing* her."

"You saw her last Tuesday night." Her voice wavered. "You took her out to dinner. She told me."

Cain swore under his breath. He should have guessed. Tiffany, making trouble as usual. "Last Tuesday night," he told her steadily, "two visiting bankers from New York invited me out to dinner. Unknown to me, they'd also invited Tiffany. She'd met them earlier in the month during a business trip to New York."

Mardi stirred in his arms and winced as the movement hurt. So Tiffany had been overseas.... *That* was why she'd been out of the picture, not because Cain had severed their relationship. Mardi blinked back bitter tears. "And you took Tiffany home after your business dinner?"

"No, Mardi. One of the bankers took her home."

She bit down on her lip. Could she believe him? If he hadn't taken Tiffany home that evening, when had he given her the bracelet? "Did you tell Tiffany you loved *her* when you gave her that diamond bracelet?"

Cain laughed. He actually laughed. "So she couldn't resist telling you that, too."

He wasn't even going to deny it! Her heart shriveled.

"Let me tell you how she came by that bracelet, Mardi." There was a steely grimness in his voice, a dangerous glint in his eye.

"You don't have to explain," she mumbled, wishing the warmth of his cradling arms and chest didn't feel so comfortable…so safe. "You never promised to love me. Or to be faithful."

He uttered a short, succinct expletive. "Mardi, just listen, please. After Sylvia's death last year I took some of her jewelry into work one day and told the partners and our secretaries to take any pieces they wanted for their wives or daughters, or to keep for themselves. The only things I kept were her wedding and engagement rings to give to Ben one day, to give to his future wife, if he wanted to."

A sardonic twist dipped the corner of his mouth. "Tiffany was at the forefront of the grabbing frenzy. It's just like her to pick the most expensive piece of the lot."

"You didn't give her the bracelet last Tuesday night?"

"Is *that* what she told you?" Cain had murderous thoughts for a second. "She's had that bracelet since the end of last year, Mardi. Any of my colleagues will verify it. Tiffany and I have never been anything but business colleagues." He pressed soothing lips to her brow. "She might have wanted more but I never did. I never wanted that kind of involvement with her."

"Never?"

"Strange as it may seem in this day and age, I believe in fidelity in marriage. I might have been a bit wild before my marriage, but not during...and not even since." As her eyes flickered under his, hope warring with skepticism, his lip quirked. "I found satisfaction in other ways, becoming even more ruthlessly obsessed with my work." He looked down at her and his eyes softened. "Now I find more satisfaction in you...in my family."

Mardi couldn't believe she was hearing the words, that his *family* gave him more satisfaction than his work or making money.

"Tiffany wants you," she said shakily.

"My darling, Tiffany can want me all she likes, it's *you* I want. I love you. Only you. Only you and our sons." The glistening tenderness in his eyes confirmed what his lips were telling her. "I never knew what love was before I met you."

His breath warmed her cheek as his words warmed her soul. "I cared for my son and wanted what was best for him," he admitted soberly, "but I didn't know how to love him. You taught me how. You've unlocked emotions I've never felt before, opened my eyes to what really matters in life."

He rocked her gently in his arms, the warm strong arms she loved to feel wrapped around her. She sank back against him, trusting him finally, and relishing every tender, revealing word he unburdened from deep down in his heart.

"You've shown me that a person's value doesn't depend on how clever or important or financially successful you are, that your worth isn't measured in terms of money or fame or ability. It goes much deeper than that." Loving fingers stroked over her cheek. "You've shown me how to relax and enjoy life, to enjoy my family."

"Oh, Cain..." She tried to tell him with her eyes that

she loved him, too, but hesitated to say it aloud, not sure he'd believe her.

"Don't try to speak. You just get better." He lifted his head as a car door banged outside. "Here's Graham. Let's see what he thinks of you."

The doctor gave her a thorough check-over and asked a lot of probing questions before helping her to her feet and checking her over some more. He seemed satisfied that she hadn't broken any bones and had only a mild case of concussion, but suggested that she have X rays if any pain persisted.

"Just keep an eye on her for a day or so," he advised Cain, and told him the danger signs to look for.

"I won't let her out of my sight," Cain promised, and his eyes were on her again now, filled with a burning tenderness.

"I'll help you carry her back to bed before I leave," Graham offered.

"I'll carry her," Cain said at once. "But by all means, check her over again when I get her up to bed." He scooped her into his arms with the utmost care and she barely felt a twinge. In her present euphoric state it would have taken another tumble down the stairs to make any pain register.

Chapter Fourteen

Cain brought the two boys into the master bedroom late Sunday morning while Mardi was having a light breakfast in bed. She'd wanted to get up, insisting she felt fine, but Cain insisted she stay put and be pampered, at least until the afternoon.

"Mummy, how did you fall down the stairs?" Nicky asked, his eyes wide with awe behind his new purple-rimmed glasses.

"You have to be careful on stairs," Ben warned, parroting Mardi's own words on past occasions.

"That's right, you do," Mardi said with feeling, giving them both a reassuring smile. "I wasn't watching what I was doing. But I'm all right now, luckily." She had bruises all over her body, and a few minor aches and pains, as well as a headache, but no serious aftereffects.

"If you want anything, I'll fetch it for you, Mummy." Nicky's eyes were still anxious. He'd never known his mother to be out of action before.

"Me, too," Ben said, wanting to be included in his new mother's care.

Mardi's heart felt so full she couldn't speak. Since her fall last night it was as if a magic wand had been waved, melting her black despair and dissolving all the doubts that had plagued her for weeks. Cain loved her, and he wasn't and never had been involved with the detestable Tiffany. She knew they would still have to see his sexy colleague from time to time, because the two worked together, but Tiffany's lies and innuendoes would no longer find their target.

Life, Mardi thought as Cain removed her breakfast tray and plumped up her pillows, couldn't get any better than this.

Later in the day she insisted on getting dressed and coming downstairs, but Cain still wouldn't allow her to do anything, settling her into the poncho-draped sofa in the family room and ordering her to stay there.

"You'd better not read or watch TV if your head's still bad," he advised. "Just relax. Lie back and think about the book you intend to write."

She raised misty eyes to his and smiled, a woman loved and in love. *Equal partners,* Cain had said once, and that was how it felt.

"Can I bring Scoots in?" Nicky asked, hoping the sight of her beloved Labrador might accelerate his mother's recovery. "He's whining to come in and see you. *Can* I, Mummy?"

"Please?" Ben begged. "Scoots is *family.*"

"Um…" Mardi glanced up at Cain. Since they'd moved into the big house, Scoots had been confined to the basement gym or the garden.

"Sure. Bring him in." Cain waved a benign hand. "As long as you don't let him jump on your mother."

"I won't!" Nicky shot off, with Ben in hot pursuit.

"You'd better check that his paws are clean," Mardi called after them.

"You won't have to worry about white carpets and couches for much longer," Cain said cryptically, and it wasn't until later, when the boys had taken Scoots out into the garden to play, that she queried the remark.

"What did you mean—I won't have to worry for much longer about the white carpets and couches?"

"Because we won't be in this house for much longer. We'll have a more suitable home soon, a more family-oriented home." Cain caught her eye as he said it, and she would have sworn he was holding his breath.

He was doing this for *her*, because he knew she wasn't suited to the glamorous lifestyle his first wife had taken to so naturally. She wasn't a social butterfly like Sylvia, who'd lived to entertain and be entertained. She was the motherly, domesticated type, not the high-society glamour-puss type.

"And Tiffany won't ever bother you again," Cain promised her. "You won't ever have to see her again."

Mardi cocked her head at him. "You're moving to another merchant bank?"

"I'm giving up merchant banking altogether."

Her jaw dropped. "But you've been so successful...and you're so good at it."

He smiled, bringing her gaze to his lips—those warm, sensual, kissable lips that she loved to taste and suck and savor. "I don't find the cutthroat world of international finance satisfying anymore—if I ever did. It's served its purpose. We're well set up financially, and we'll be selling this property, of course, which has leapt in value since I bought it. We can afford to take a risk."

"A risk?" What *was* he talking about? There was a glimmer of excitement in his eyes, even a reckless glint.

"I intend to move to the country to live—if you'll agree to it." Cain paused, gratified at the way her eyes lit up. "I want to bring up our boys in a more healthy, natural environment, among people who value more basic things in life than money and possessions and their position on the social scale. I have a feeling it's what you want, too."

He'd kept his dream under wraps until he'd been sure that Mardi wasn't going to eagerly embrace the glossy, fast-living world that Sylvia had reveled in. But she hadn't, as he'd known in his heart she wouldn't. A life of luxury and an entrée into high society would never have seduced or corrupted Mardi. The superficial life of wealth and power that he'd once craved himself—and succeeded in, far beyond his wildest expectations—meant nothing to her and never would. Just as it no longer meant anything to him.

Mardi swallowed as she looked up at him. "Oh, Cain, if you're doing this for me—"

"I'm doing it for all of us. It's something I've been thinking about for some time. Since my business trip to the Hunter Valley a few weeks ago."

The Hunter Valley. Ah yes, she remembered that trip.

"While I was there, I heard about a property that was to come up for sale in the near future, and I took a look at it. It was on the banks of the Hunter River—a beautiful spot. It had stud cattle and a large vineyard. There's a house, too, of course. A very comfortable, rambling family home. I was sure you and the boys would love it."

He paused, hoping the stunned expression in her eyes was a good sign. "The moment I saw it, the pieces of my life started to fall into place like a jigsaw puzzle that I hadn't been able to put together. I knew what I wanted to do with my life, with my future—*our* future. I wanted to own and run a property just like that. *That* one, if I was able to buy it. It's now on the market and I have first option to buy.''

"You intend to run a *vineyard*? And breed *cattle*?" Mardi tried not to sound too incredulous, or to show any doubt in her eyes. "You told me once that you'd only ever been interested in figures and finance and mathematics. Have you ever *been* on a farm? Or *worked* on a farm?" Inside, her heart was beating overtime, with sheer exhilaration at the prospect.

"I have, actually. When I was a boy we lived a bike ride away from a sheep farm in New Zealand. After my mother died, I spent a lot of my spare time at the farm, mostly to get away from my stepmother, but also to get away from my father—though he was away from home a lot of the time, playing cricket. I worked there after school and at weekends. It was an escape, but I loved it, too. I'm not afraid of hard physical work, Mardi. I'm not afraid to get my hands dirty.''

Mardi smiled. No, she knew he wasn't.

"With the money and investments I've made and my financial expertise, I should be able to make a go of it—as long as you're with me, my darling.'' Cain trailed warm fingers down her bare arm.

"Oh, Cain, I'll be behind you all the way.'' Her skin tingled under his touch. Her headache and all her other aches and pains had vanished.

"I didn't doubt that you would.'' He found her hand and gave it a squeeze. "It'll be hard going, but I'm sure we'll all relish the life. It'll be a great place to bring up the boys—all those wide-open spaces and the fresh country air. There's a good primary school, by the way, in a town quite close by.''

Bemused, she recalled how Cain had sung the praises of

St. Mark's private school, about what a great school it was. It was why Darrell had been determined to send Nicky there, even paying his son's school fees in advance. *If* he'd paid them. She'd begun to wonder, since learning how much money her late husband had squandered on Sylvia Templar and how little he'd cared about his family, if *Cain* could have secretly paid those fees, to make sure she sent Nicky back to St. Mark's with Ben—it would be just the kind of thing he would do. But that question could wait.

"You won't mind taking Ben out of St. Mark's?" she asked instead.

"Not a problem. We can always send the boys back there when they reach senior school, if we think it would be best for them. We'd have to be prepared to let them board, or else move back to Sydney ourselves. But if we decide we want to stay in the Hunter Valley, there are other private schools that would be closer to us. Let's just wait and see. That decision won't arise for a few years."

He seemed to have thought of everything. "It sounds wonderful," she said, dreamy-eyed. A new house, a brand-new lifestyle, a challenging, healthy environment for the boys. A *real* world…a world she could embrace with enthusiasm.

"I don't want you to give up on your plan to write a book." Cain kissed her on the lips, letting his mouth linger a moment before going on. "And don't say you won't have time… I'll make sure you'll still have adequate help in the house."

The feel of his lips on hers scattered her thoughts for a second, the warmth of his mouth sending the same thrill through her as always, the same hot wave of delicious sensation. And then his words penetrated.

"*Elena's* coming with us?" She tried to imagine the taciturn housekeeper in a rustic country house and failed.

Elena was so fastidious about the state of the house, so disapproving when a single thing was out of place. She'd been well trained by Sylvia to maintain the most impeccable standards and to stay aloof. She wasn't a comfortable person to be around.

Cain chuckled at the look on her face. "No, not Elena. We'll find someone local after we move in. You can choose her yourself. Someone who's not too gossipy, so you can concentrate on your writing."

"A lot of husbands wouldn't be so…supportive." She gazed up at him with a grateful, rather pensive smile.

"I'll be behind you every step of the way, my love, when I'm not racing you off to the bedroom." Cain nuzzled his rough jaw into the warm hollow of her throat. He'd been too concerned about her to bother shaving today.

"Actually, I'm toying with the idea of taking on another job myself," he confessed, "when I'm not laboring in the vineyard or breeding cattle. There's a need for experienced types like me to give financial advice to people who seek help. I could answer questions over the Internet while you're writing books. It would keep my skills alive and my mind active and bring in some extra income, hopefully. Until you become a bestselling author and I won't need to work ever again."

She laughed, and shook her head. Somehow she no longer felt the same burning need to write as she had only the day before. There were so many other possibilities and challenges lying ahead. But she knew the urge would come back—it always did.

"How are you feeling?" Cain asked, drawing back to search her face. "How's your head? I haven't tired you, have I?"

"*Tired* me! You've *invigorated* me." She reached up

and curled her arms round his neck. "Our future sounds like a dream."

"It's no dream, Mardi," Cain murmured against her upturned lips. "Unless it's a dream come true."

"It is." Her eyes shone. "I love you, Cain." The words were muffled as his lips covered hers. "I love you with all my heart." He, too, had turned into a dream come true.

Epilogue

As the Qantas 747 touched down at Auckland airport, Mardi could sense Cain's tension. He'd only come to New Zealand for her sake—and for Ben's.

But he'd stuck to his promise to make the trip during the school holidays, before their move to the Hunter Valley. He'd refused to let his parents know they were coming. "They'd only get in a flap or tell us not the bother. Best if we just turn up."

They hired a car to Cain's parents' home. Since his father had retired some years ago, the couple had lived in a small modern unit in a bayside suburb, closer to the city than their original family home had been.

Above them the clouds were low and dark, like Cain's mood.

His stepmother, Brenda, answered the door. She was a small, wiry, thin-lipped woman with a close-cropped cap of silver-gray hair. When she saw Cain she visibly stiffened. "What are *you* doing here?"

"Hullo to you, too, Brenda," Cain said. "Is my father at home?"

"Your father's sick."

"And you didn't think to let me know?"

His stepmother said, "He didn't want anyone to know. You know what the media's like when anyone famous is reported ill. They start writing your obituary, and reporters camp outside your front gate like vultures. He's not on his last legs yet."

Mardi could understand Sherman Templar wanting his privacy. He was a legend in this country...New Zealand's most famous international cricketer of all time.

"How sick is he?" Cain rasped.

"He has the flu. And bronchitis. He's asleep." Brenda didn't budge, making no move to invite them in. "You should have let us know you were coming."

"So you could tell me not the come?" Cain arched a cynical eyebrow.

An irate shout came from inside the house. "Who's at the door, Brenda? There's a draught coming in. Want me to catch pneumonia?"

Cain ushered his wife and sons past his stepmother into the front room. His father was sitting in a high-backed armchair in the far corner, with a rug over his knees. His hair was whiter, his shoulders more hunched than the last time Cain had seen him, but his craggy face and sharp blue eyes showed no sign of mortal sickness.

"*You!*" Sherman sounded no more welcoming than his wife. He glanced at Mardi and the two boys, then frowned at Cain. "You've ditched your flashy society wife?"

Cain slipped his arm round Mardi's waist. "Sylvia died last year, Father. This is Mardi. We married a month ago. And her son Nicky—*our* son now." He waved the two boys forward. "You remember Ben, Father?"

Ben marched boldly forward. "Are you my grandpa? Dad says I've met you before but I don't 'member."

"You were too little to remember." Sherman's voice was gruff. Maybe it was the bronchitis, Mardi thought. Or maybe he actually felt something for his grandson.

Ben handed a small round package to Sherman, wrapped in gold foil. "This is for you, Grandpa. I made it myself."

"I hope it's not chocolates." Brenda spoke up from behind. "He's not allowed to have chocolates."

"I don't know how to make choc'lates," Ben assured her solemnly. "Go on, Grandpa. Open it."

He did. "A ball?" He rolled it over in his wrinkled hands. "A *cricket* ball?"

"It's not a real cricket ball," Ben conceded. "It's made of papier-mâché. It won't break anything in the house, like a real cricket ball would. We can play a game of catchy if you like."

"Cain told him you used to play cricket, Mr. Templar," Mardi explained.

"He did, did he?" The old man seemed gratified that his son had remembered his past glory. "You like cricket, Ben?"

"Sherman, don't you start throwing balls around in the house." Brenda's sharp voice intruded.

Mardi was quick to deflect any discord. "Nicky and I have something for you, too, Mr. Templar. You first, Nicky."

Nicky stepped forward, thrusting a roughly wrapped package of his own into the old man's hands. "Mummy said you might like a photo of us," he said. "'Cause we live a long way away and we never see you."

As Sherman accepted the gift and pulled aside the brightly colored wrapping, Nicky spoke up again. "I chose the paper and wrapped it myself. Joe took the photo—he's our gardener—and Mummy bought the frame.''

Sherman looked down at the framed photograph for a long moment. In the silence, his chest wheezed. ''Your family looks happy,'' he said finally, and speared a glance up at Cain. ''Happier than you looked when you came home four years ago.''

Cain's eyes flickered, surprised that his father would have noticed or cared how he'd looked or felt. ''I am happier,'' he said, his hand tightening on Mardi's waist. ''I've found what I want now.''

''Is that so? You gave the impression you'd found what you wanted four years ago, when you turned up after all those years away to flaunt your glamorous trophy wife and your well-bred baby and to boast about your—''

''Boys, why don't we pop outside and take a look at the garden?'' Mardi cut in, not wanting the children to hear this. ''Come on, I'll take you.''

''Brenda, *you* take them.'' Cain held on to his wife as she tried to step away. ''I want Mardi here with me.'' *Where she belongs,* he let his eyes tell them.

Brenda's mouth thinned even further. ''It's time you left. You're tiring Sherman. I don't want him upset. He's a sick man, remember.''

''Take the boys outside, Brenda,'' Sherman commanded. ''We need to talk.''

His wife looked taken aback, as if he'd never spoken like that to her before. Maybe he hadn't, Mardi mused. Maybe he'd allowed Brenda to call all the shots in the past, and his wife was the person most responsible for the rift between father and son—and for keeping it alive all this time. From what she'd gathered from Cain, his stepmother had always resented him, fearing, perhaps, that Cain would take his father's affection away from her own children.

Sherman waited until they'd left the room, then said, "Yeah, you were full of yourself back then, and what you'd achieved with your life. You hadn't come home to see *me*, you'd come home to gloat."

He gave a wheezing cough, but it didn't stop him. "But I could see that all your money and success hadn't satisfied you or made you a contented man. You wanted more. *She* wanted more. I was glad when you took your family back to where you came from. I could see you were on the road to hell."

Cain sucked in his breath, his father's words shaking him. "*That's* why you lashed out at me? Because you thought I was on the road to hell?"

The old man shrugged. "My sporting career gave me a great deal of personal happiness, a sense of real personal achievement. I'd hoped for the same for you."

A hint of that disappointment glimmered briefly. "When you left New Zealand I despaired of you. How many filthy rich, driven men end up happy and satisfied with their lives? I had deep misgivings. And my fears were justified when you came home four years ago...."

Cain's lips parted, but he refrained from comment when Mardi pressed his hand to let the old man finish.

"It was obvious—" his father's brow lowered at the memory "—that your brilliant career in high finance and all the millions you'd made and your glossy society marriage hadn't given you an iota of genuine satisfaction or happiness. As far as I was concerned, you'd sold your soul to the devil."

Cain was looking at his father as if seeing him for the first time. "You were right. It wasn't what I'd been looking for. It just took me a while to realize it."

Sherman threw his rug aside and hauled himself to his feet. 'You've changed." He touched his son's arm—something he hadn't done since Cain was a small boy. "Did *she* change you? Your new wife?" He glanced at Mardi with real warmth in his eyes, a warmth he then turned on his son. "I'm glad you've found what you've been looking for, boy. That you've finally found some real happiness in your life."

"So am I," Cain said with feeling, and for the first time in years he actually smiled at his father, wanting finally to dissolve the years of bitterness and misunderstanding. His father had cared about him after all. Perhaps he'd even felt some love for him. He just hadn't been able to show it.

"So am I," he repeated, reaching for Mardi. "I have the right woman now, and two healthy sons—a family I love," he said, using the word he'd never been able to say in the past. "And my wife and I are about to embark on brand-new careers in the Hunter Valley. We've bought a vineyard and cattle stud. While I'm busy with those, Mardi's going to write books."

Sherman looked so wobbly for a second that Cain had to reach out to steady him. "You'd better sit down again, Father. Brenda will kill me if you get any worse."

"I won't get any worse," Sherman growled. But he sank down in his armchair. "Now grab a chair yourselves and tell me everything. But before you do, I want you to know that I'm proud of you, Cain." It was quite an admission for Sherman Templar.

"You'd better wait and see if I can make a success of my new life," Cain said wryly.

"That's not why I'm proud of you." The old man had to stop for a moment to give a wheezing cough. "It's because you've become the kind of son I can be proud of— whether you succeed in your new career or not." He glanced at the carefully wrapped parcel in Mardi's hand and said gruffly, as if to diffuse all the emotion flowing around, "You've brought something for me, too, you said?"

"Well, it's just something I knitted for you, Mr. Templar." Mardi handed him the gift she'd been holding all this time. "I thought it might come in handy in the winter."

Sherman peeled back the silver wrapping and pulled out a soft mohair scarf in shades of gray and pale blue. "*You* knitted this for me?" There was a faint sparkle in his eyes. "People usually bring me things you can buy without any effort, like flowers or chocolates." He picked up the papier-mâché cricket ball and the framed photograph and looked down at them. "All these gifts have taken time and effort. And a lot of loving thought. Thank you."

"I'm sorry I didn't make you something myself." Cain gave a rueful smile. He hadn't even wanted to come. *Wouldn't* have come, but for Mardi. Another debt he owed her.

Sherman raised misty eyes to his son. "You've given me a very special gift," the old man said huskily. "You've given me back my son."

Cain leaned forward and gripped his father's shoulder. "That works both ways. Don't talk anymore, Father. It's making you cough. We'll go now and come back again tomorrow. We're here for three days. Then we have to go home and start moving house."

Mardi, watching father and son, felt sure her heart would burst from the sheer happiness she felt. For Cain, especially. Now he would have no more dark shadows to haunt him. And no matter what happened in the future, they would have each other. They would *all* have each other.

*   *   *   *   *

**Where royalty and romance
go hand in hand...**

The series continues in Silhouette Romance
with these unforgettable novels:

HER ROYAL HUSBAND
by Cara Colter
on sale July 2002 (SR #1600)

THE PRINCESS HAS AMNESIA!
by Patricia Thayer
on sale August 2002 (SR #1606)

SEARCHING FOR HER PRINCE
by Karen Rose Smith
on sale September 2002 (SR #1612)

And look for more Crown and Glory stories in
SILHOUETTE DESIRE starting in October 2002!

Available at your favorite retail outlet.

Silhouette®
Where love comes alive™

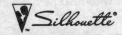

COMING NEXT MONTH